CAPTURED!

There had been two shots.

Two shots blending as one.

"Hickok!" Blade exclaimed, and surged toward the west bank, stepping past Achilles, and even as he moved there were two more shots. "Let's go!"

A large, vague shape suddenly came into view on the left, angling to intercept them.

"Blade!" Achilles cried in warning.

"I see it," the giant replied, and aimed the Commando on the run. He squeezed the trigger, shooting by instinct, and his aim turned out to be unerring.

The thing clutched at its torso and toppled.

Blade faced front, his legs pounding, his heart doing the same. What if he was too late? What if the mutations had killed his friends and the others? What if his blunder wound up costing lives, the lives of the two best friends he had?

Other books in the *Endworld* series:

#23:
YELLOWSTONE RUN

DAVID ROBBINS

LEISURE BOOKS   NEW YORK CITY

Dedicated to . . .
Judy, Joshua, and Shane.

To Charlene, Wayne, Troy, and Jason,
in friendship.

And to *KONA, MONARCH OF MONSTER ISLE*.
For the thrills.

A LEISURE BOOK®

September 1990

Published by

Dorchester Publishing Co., Inc.
276 Fifth Avenue
New York, NY 10001

Printed in the United States of America.

PROLOGUE

There was something out there.

Something lurking in the tall timber.

Eagle Feather paused in the act of chopping wood for the fire, his right arm upraised, his tomahawk gleaming in the afternoon sunlight, and gazed at the surrounding forest, his keen brown eyes scrutinizing every shadow. The feeling of being watched was stronger now than ever before, and he frowned when he failed to detect any movement in the pine trees.

"Is something wrong?"

Putting a smile on his face, Eagle Feather turned at the sound of his wife's melodious voice and looked at the woman he loved more than life itself. "What could be wrong?" he responded, hoping he conveyed a lighthearted attitude. He didn't want to worry Morning Dew or the children. Yet.

"I don't know," she said uncertainly, staring at the woods. "You seem troubled."

Eagle Feather lowered the tomahawk and pretended to inspect its edge. "You are imagining things."

"If you say so," Morning Dew said, and returned to the

task of preparing the fish their sons had caught an hour ago for their supper. She glanced at him once reproachfully.

Knowing that his wife of 12 years could intuitively sense when he was troubled, and annoyed at himself for not confiding in her, Eagle Feather continued to trim the limbs he had collected, removing the thinner stems to be used as kindling and chopping the larger branches into manageable sections. He strained his ears to catch the slightest sound from the forest, but all he heard were birds and squirrels and the whispering of the breeze. How could he justify alarming Morning Dew when all he had to go on was a vague feeling?

Youthful laughter filled the air, and a moment later two boys came running around the family tipi, which was situated on the north bank of the gently flowing stream, and halted, giggling and shoving one another.

Straightening, Eagle Feather smiled at his sons. The oldest, Little Mountain, was ten years old. Black Elk, who strongly resembled his mother, was only eight. "What are you two up to?"

"We want to go hunt deer," Little Mountain declared.

"Hunt deer," Black Elk echoed, nodding vigorously.

"We already have fish for our meal. We don't need a deer," Eagle Feather said, resolving to keep his sons close to the camp.

"But mother said I could have new moccasins," Little Mountain stated, squaring his slim shoulders.

"Me too," Black Elk added.

"I want you to play near our camp," Eagle Feather told them.

"But there's nothing to do here," Little Mountain protested.

"I can find something for you to do," Eagle Feather commented sternly.

"I thought we were supposed to have fun," Little Mountain said, clearly disappointed, and sighed.

Eagle Feather became aware of his wife's intent scrutiny, and he decided to compromise before she grew even more suspicious. He *had* promised the boys this would be a fun-filled trip to the old National Park, and he saw a way to kill two birds with one stone, to allay his fears and ensure the forest was safe for the boys. "I'll tell you what. You finish chopping this wood, and when I come back you can go deer hunting."

"Where are you going, Father?" Black Elk asked.

"To find a handful of leaves."

"What?" the boy responded, puzzled. His older brother whispered in his ear and they both laughed.

"Here," Eagle Feather said, and handed the tomahawk to Little Mountain. "Try not to cut your foot off."

"I won't," Little Mountain replied, eagerly grabbing the handle.

Deliberately avoiding his wife's gaze, Eagle Feather walked to their tipi and went inside to retrieve his Winchester. He emerged, worked the lever to insert a round into the chamber, and headed for the woods.

"Be careful," Morning Dew advised.

Eagler Feather looked back at her and nodded. "Always. Keep your rifle handy in case a bear should show up. I saw grizzly sign yesterday."

"I'll keep a sharp watch," she promised.

Cradling his Winchester, Eagle Feather advanced into the trees, entering a somber domain of shadows and dank scents, where his footsteps padded noiselessly on the matted carpet of pine needles and spongy vegetation. This area of the ancient wonderland, bordering the Lamar Valley, was always verdant in the summer and early fall. Spruce, Douglas fir, and lodgepole pine were especially numerous. A scratching noise came from overhead, and he gazed up to observe a Steller's jay hopping from limb to limb. Like most of the wildlife they had encountered, the big blue and black bird displayed no fear at his presence.

Pressing onward, Eagle Feather penetrated deeper into the forest, traveling 50 yards from the camp. He saw several sparrows, a red squirrel, and a jackrabbit. The rabbit bounded away, performing fifteen-foot leaps with ease, but otherwise the animals were going about their daily business and not displaying any agitation whatsoever. And surely, Eagle Feather reasoned, there would be an undercurrent of unrest in the forest if danger was present.

Perhaps *he* was imagining things, not Morning Dew.

Maybe spotting those grizzly tracks had unnerved him more than he knew. Maybe, since they were so far from Kalispell and home, since they were alone in an uninhabited wilderness, he was allowing unfounded apprehension to get the better of him. After all, he had spent most of his life as a hunter and a trapper. He knew all the habits of the animals in the woods. None of them, even the grizzly, were unduly menacing if a person used common sense and took adequate precautions. Most animals wisely shied away from man.

Except for the mutations.

The thought troubled him. If there were mutations in the Park, then his family was in grave jeopardy. But as far as he knew, neither a nuclear missile nor a chemical-warfare weapon had struck within hundreds of miles of the area. The Park had survived World War Three virtually unscathed. And without the radiation or chemical toxins to poison and derange the entire biological chain, the likelihood of mutations flourishing was extremely slim.

Eagle Feather skirted a tree and halted on the rim of a low rise. Thirty feet below lay an oval spring. Curious, wanting to taste the water to determine if it was as good as the delicious stream water, he walked down the gentle slope. A six-inch strip of soft, muddy earth ringed the spring, and he knelt next to the strip and sank his left hand under the surface to scoop some water to his mouth.

Only then did he see the tracks.

Puzzled, he froze with his hand halfway to his lips, and regarded the pair of unique prints in the mud to his left. They were the strangest prints he'd ever seen, a curious combination of human and bestial traits. Approximately 14 inches in length and six inches wide, they resembled a naked human footprint except for the fact that each toe had a four-inch nail similar to the typical claw on the toe of a bear. He let the water trickle from his palm and reached out to touch the track. From the softness of the mud and the cohesive texture of the print, he judged that the pair had been made within the last 30 minutes. Suddenly his mind blared a warning.

Strange prints?

Combination of human and bestial traits?

Eagle Feather straightened and turned from the spring, and even as he rotated a piercing scream rent the tranquility of the forest, coming from the direction of the tipi.

Morning Dew and the boys!

A wave of fear washed over him, and Eagle Feather sprinted up the slope and took off at full speed toward the camp, vaulting logs and low-lying boulders, darting around the bigger obstacles, his blood racing faster than his feet.

More screams sounded, the unmistakable cries of the boys.

Eagle Feather fairly flew over the terrain, oblivious to the limbs and brush that snatched at his buckskins and scratched his skin. He realized that he'd been right all along, that there had been something in the woods, a mutation, one of the vile creatures despised by his entire tribe, by every Flathead Indian. Mutations were a blight on the planet, a consequence of the white man tampering with forces better left alone. The Flatheads killed each mutation they found, and large tracts of the former state of Montana had been cleared of the repulsive horrors.

The screaming abruptly ceased.

No! Eagle Feather shrieked in his mind, and he goaded his flagging muscles to increased speed. He'd already covered 40 yards. The tipi should be in sight at any moment. Seconds later he saw the camp and his breath caught in his throat.

Someone or something had torn the tipi down, had ripped the buffalo hide to ribbons and snapped the support poles into pieces. Their personal effects had been torn apart and scattered all about. The horses, which had been tied to the left of the tipi, were gone. And there wasn't a living soul in sight.

Eagle Feather dashed into the ruined camp and halted, glancing wildly around for his wife and sons. He spied her rifle lying in the grass to his right, its stock splintered. The attack must have occurred so swiftly that she had been unable to get off a single shot. Frantic, he began hunting for tracks, for blood, for any sign to tell him what had happened to his family. On the bank of the stream he found the clue he needed.

Strange tracks, exactly like those at the spring, the toes pointing to the south, were clearly visible.

Eagle Feather plunged into the knee-high water and quickly crossed to the far side. There, distinct in the damp earth in the water's edge, were more of the tracks, lots more, all heading to the south.

What *were* they?

He ran into the forest, his gaze glued to the ground, seeking tracks or partial prints, anything to indicate the specific direction the things had taken. After 20 yards he found a footprint angling to the southwest and he sprinted in that direction. A vague recollection gnawed at his mind, and he experienced a peculiar feeling that he should know what the things were he pursued.

The creatures were still bearing to the southwest.

Eagle Feather had no way of estimating their rate of travel. He hoped—he prayed—he could overtake them before nightfall. Since he hadn't seen any blood or discovered any bodies, he derived comfort from knowing Morning Dew, Little Thunder, and Black Elk were probably still alive.

But who, or what, had abducted them? And why?

The minutes dragged by. Eagle Feather's leg muscles began to ache, but he ignored the discomfort. He had no intention of resting until he caught up with his family. Why, he berated himself, had he ever taken them so far from Kalispell? Why had he ventured outside of Flathead territory? Technically speaking, northwestern Wyoming was part of the Civilized Zone, and the Civilized Zone and the Flatheads were allies in the Federation. But no one lived in the Park anymore. Anyone with half a brain preferred to live closer to civilization, or what was left of it 106 years after the nuclear holocaust.

Eagle Feather glanced up at the sun, estimating the time remaining until dark. It was only the first week of September, so he would have four or five hours of daylight left in which to rescue his loved ones.

The trees began to thin out, and the countryside became rockier and intersected with deep gorges, affording plenty of places to hide. The rocky soil would make tracking a lot more difficult.

Frustrated, Eagle Feather cast about for additional tracks.

Part of a heel stood out near a scrawny shrub.

Eagle Feather's eyes narrowed. The devils had changed direction again and were now bearing to the southwest. Why were they altering their course so frequently? Did they know he was after them? Were they striving to shake him off their trail, or was this typical of their behavior? He spotted a ravine up ahead, toward which the tracks appeared to be heading, and he tightened his hold on the Winchester.

The ravine was a perfect site for an ambush.

Twenty feet from the gap in the rocks he abruptly stopped, his skin tingling, his eyes on the strip of buckskin blouse lying two yards away.

Morning Dew!

He dashed to the strip and scooped the soft material into his left hand, examining it closely. There could be no doubt. The material had been ripped from the shoulder of Morning Dew's blouse. Rage made him grip the buckskin until his knuckles turned white, and then he tucked the strip under his belt and hastened into the ravine.

On both sides reared towering walls of rock. Perched on the top were boulders of different sizes, ranging from a few feet in diameter to gigantic slabs ten feet across.

His prudence dashed to bits by the finding of the material, Eagle Feather jogged 25 feet into the steep-sided ravine before he awoke to his mistake. He halted and gazed up at the rim, then back at the opening, and decided he was being foolish. If he acted rashly, if he was killed, who would save those he held most dear?

A small stone clattered down from high above.

Eagler Feather looked up, and his veins seemed to transform into ice when he beheld the hulking, bearish figures on the brink of the ravine, perhaps 30 yards distant on the right-hand side. They were too far up, and the curve of the rock wall served to obstruct his view, so he couldn't see them plainly. He glimpsed a dozen huge, hairy forms milling about the rim, heard a rumbling noise, and then the boulders started to fall.

They were causing a rock slide!

Eagle Feather took one look at the avalanche of boulders and rocks hurtling toward the bottom of the ravine, and whirled. He darted toward the opening, his ears registering the mighty crash of the larger boulders as they struck the stone walls and slammed to the ground. The whole ravine reverberated with the din. Several boulders thudded down within a few feet of his flying heels, and the ground itself shook.

A rock smacked against his left shoulder.

The opening was now only six feet away. He took another stride, then leaped, his arms outstretched, the Winchester in his right hand. A heavy object rammed against his legs, but an instant later he was out of the gap and tumbling a few yards to slam up against a stunted tree. He shoved erect and stared in horror at the boulders and rocks now blocking the gap, tons and tons of stone no one could budge.

They had cut him off from his family!

Eagle Feather stepped to the left, intending to seek a way around the ravine, when a chilling sound wafted down from overhead, the sound of deep, guttural laughter, echoing from wall to wall, mocking him, making him realize the bearish figures had just been toying with him.

Bearish figures?

Suddenly the amorphous memory that had eluded him solidified with startling clarity, and Eagle Feather knew the identity of the creatures. The knowledge swamped him in an emotional mire of sheer terror. He gaped at the rim, thinking of his beloved wife and sons in the clutches of those fiends, and shivered.

CHAPTER ONE

"Daddy?"

"Hmmmmm ?"

"I think I have a nibble."

The lean man attired in buckskins opened his blue eyes and gazed idly at the bobber attached to his son's fishing line, which dangled in the moat not two yards from their feet. "Are you sure?"

"Yep. I saw the bobber move," the boy stated with a conviction belying his almost five years of age.

Sighing, the man sat up and stretched. He ran his right hand through his blond hair, then stroked his blond mustache. "Why don't you reel in your line slowly," he advised. "Let's take a gander at what you've hooked."

"A what?"

"A gander. That means to take a look."

"Mom's right," Ringo said, starting to turn the reel. Like his father, he wore buckskins. Like his father, he had blond hair and striking blue eyes. Unlike his father, he did *not* wear a pair of pearl-handled Colt Python revolvers around his waist.

"What's your mom right about?" the gunman asked.

"She was talking to Uncle Geronimo the other night."

"Uh-oh."

"And I heard what they said," Ringo disclosed, carefully drawing the line into the reel.

The gunman leaned toward his son. "What did they say?"

"I can't tell you."

"Why the blazes not?"

"Because it's a secret," Ringo said, and grinned.

Leaning back on his elbows, the gunman regarded the boy critically. "Well, this is a fine how-do-you-do."

Ringo stopped reeling and stared at his dad. "A what?"

"A how-do-you-do. It's something that happens that you don't want to happen."

The boy grinned. "Yep. Uncle Geronimo has the right idea."

"What did that mangy Injun say?"

"I can't tell you. It's a secret."

"Are you tellin' me that your mom and Uncle Geronimo are both in on the same secret?"

Ringo smiled. "Yep."

"It really gets my goat when those two gang up on me."

"I wish I could tell you what they said, but I promised Mom I wouldn't."

"That's okay, son," the gunman said. "If you gave your word, then I expect you to keep it. Always remember that a man is only as good as his word. I pride myself on the fact that I've never broken mine."

"Never?"

"Never. So if you don't want to tell me, that's okay. If you'd rather let your Uncle Geronimo make my life miserable again, that's okay. And if you'd rather hurt my feelings than break your word, I understand."

Ringo lowered his fishing pole and stared at his father for several seconds. "Do you want me to tell you their secret?"

"What do you think?"

"You've always told me to keep my promises."

"So?"

"So I think you're trying to trick me to see if I'll break my word," Ringo declared.

"You think I'm testin' you?"

"Yep."

The man in buckskins grinned. "You know what, sprout?"

"What?"

"You're right."

A new voice unexpectedly intruded into their conversation, coming from behind the gunman. "You had me worried for a minute there, Hickok. I thought you were trying to lay a guilt trip on your own son."

In a fluid motion the blond man stood and pivoted, his hands on his hips, an exaggerated scowl twisting his handsome countenance. He glared at the newcomer, a stocky Indian wearing a green shirt and pants constructed from the remnants of a canvas tent. The Indian's hair was black, his eyes brown. "What the dickens is this about my missus and you havin' some sort of secret, Geronimo?"

"Ringo spoke the truth," Geronimo admitted, walking toward them. "He always does. Takes after Sherry, I guess." He smirked impishly.

"I'll have you know I tell the truth all the time," Hickok said defensively.

"Oh, you tell the truth, all right. You just expand it in the process."

"Oh, yeah? Like when?"

"Like recently when you were bitten by that spider in Cincinnati," Geronimo mentioned, halting next to the gunman on the bank of the sluggishly flowing moat.

"What about it?" Hickok demanded.

"Well, I heard that you told some of the kids the spider weighed eighty pounds."

"He told *me* ninety pounds," Ringo chimed in.

"Was that all?" Geronimo responded, and chuckled. "The thing keeps growing by leaps and bounds." He beamed at Hickok. "As I recall, you originally told Blade and me that the spider was the size of your hand and didn't weigh more than five ounces."

Hickok shrugged. "I wanted the young'uns to enjoy the story. It wouldn't have been as exciting if they knew how puny the blamed spider really was."

"But a ninety-pound spider?" Geronimo said. "I'm surprised the mutation didn't squash you to a pulp when it jumped on you." He suddenly adopted a serious expression and snapped his fingers. "But I almost forgot! The thing landed on your head! No wonder you survived."

"You know, pard," Hickok commented sarcastically, "you'd be a really funny guy if you ever develop a sense of humor."

"Say, Dad?" Ringo interrupted.

"What is it?" the gunman responded, still glaring at Geronimo.

"Why are those two snakes trying to steal my line?"

Hickok swung toward the moat, his hands drifting to his Colts at the sight of a pair of slim black heads near his son's fishing line. Both heads were within an inch of one another, and the head closest to the line was actually biting at the filament. "What the devil?" he blurted out.

Geronimo, his brow furrowed, walked to the edge of the bank and squatted, peering at the reptiles.

"Should I reel in the line?" Ringo asked.

"Go ahead," Hickok directed.

The boy began turning the crank quickly, and almost immediately the sinker and the hook rose out of the water, the two snake heads rising with the line, revealing a surprising spectacle. "Golly!" he blurted out.

"What did you use for bait?" Geronimo quipped.

Hickok stepped to the water for a better view. "One of your old socks," he rejoined.

There turned out to be three snake heads, each with a neck approximately five inches long, and all attached to the same body. The first head continued to bite at the fishing line while the second head hung almost limp. Lower down, the third head had clamped its mouth on the belly of the fish Ringo had caught and was holding fast despite the fact it could never hope to swallow its prey.

"It's a mutant," Ringo said.

"It sure is," Geronimo confirmed. "I've seen two-headed animals before, but this is the first one I've seen with three heads."

"It's neat. I want to catch it and take it home to show my mom."

"Forget it," Hickok stated.

"Ahhh, gee. Why?"

"Because your ma isn't partial to creepy-crawlies, and we're not going to have this critter traipsin' all over our cabin."

"Huh?"

"Your father said no," Geronimo translated.

"He's no fun," Ringo muttered.

"Tell me about it," Geronimo mumbled in response.

"Swing the line near the bank and Uncle Geronimo will take the snake off," Hickok instructed his son.

Geronimo glanced at the gunman. "Why me?"

"You're the one who thinks he's the great expert on nature. You're the one who's always tellin' me he knows more about wild critters than I could ever hope to learn."

"True. But why me?"

"You're an Indian."

Geronimo's eyes narrowed. "What's that have to do with anything?"

"Everybody knows that Indians have a way with animals."

"True again," Geronimo said, and grinned. "I am *your* best friend."

Listening to the adults, frowning because he couldn't take the snake home, Ringo sighed and gazed to the south at the compound, his eyes brightening when he spied the giant walking toward them. "Hey, here comes Uncle Blade!"

Hickok twisted and regarded the seven-foot-tall titan for a moment. "We've got to get rid of that snake fast."

"How come, Dad?" Ringo queried.

"Don't you remember? I've told you about how Blade's dad was killed by a mutant ten years ago. Ever since, he's been right irritable around the varmints."

"I'll take it off the line," Geronimo offered.

"There's a better way," Hickok said.

"There is?"

"Yep."

Geronimo saw the gunman's jaw stiffen and knew what was coming. He stuck a finger in each ear.

"Cover your ears too, son," Hickok directed.

"What about my fishing pole?"

"Give it to me," Hickok said, and took the handle in his left hand. He looked back once at Blade, who was still 20 yards distant, then faced the moat and chuckled. "This is for Blade's dad," he declared, and drew his right Python, his arm a literal blur, his practiced hand sweeping the Colt up and out. The .357 Magnum boomed three times in swift succession, the shots almost cracking as one, and with each squeeze of the trigger a snake head erupted in a shower of skin, flesh, and eyeballs. In the space of a heartbeat all three heads were gone and the body was sliding back into the moat. "Piece of cake," he stated, and twirled the Python into its holster.

"Wow! You must be the fastest man alive!" Ringo said proudly.

"Is there any doubt?" Hickok replied.

"Not bad for an amateur," Geronimo remarked, lowering his arms and standing, his left hand brushing the tomahawk tucked under his brown leather belt.

"Amateur!" Hickok said, and snorted. "I'd like to see you give it a try."

"I can't. You shot all the heads."

"Can I have my pole?" Ringo asked, staring at the fish still attached to the hook. Part of its stomach was missing.

"Sure. Here," Hickok responded, and gave th pole back. He hooked his thumbs in his gunbelt, turned sideways, and beamed at the approaching giant.

"Do you think he has another mission for us?" Geronimo wondered.

"I hope so. I'm itchy for some action."

"The itching is from your fleas."

"Are you going to leave the Home again?" Ringo inquired while reeling in the line.

"I don't know," Hickok said. "Could be."

"Mom, Chastity, and I don't like it when you go away so much."

"I know, son. But it can't be helped. I'm a Warrior, and when the Family is threatened I have to protect everyone."

"Maybe another Warrior could go with Uncle Blade," Ringo suggested. "How about Rikki or Yama or Ares or Sundance?"

"The decision is up to Blade," Hickok said. "You know that."

"I don't think you have to worry about your dad leaving right this moment," Geronimo mentioned.

"Why not?" Ringo inquired.

"Because Blade is smiling."

The giant waved at them and nodded at the moat. "What are you doing, Nathan? *Shooting* the fish now?"

"Everybody is a comedian lately," Hickok grumbled, and returned the wave. "Nope. Just gettin' in a little target practice."

Blade reached them and halted. Every inch of his enormous frame was packed with layer after layer of rippling, bulging muscle. His dark hair hung in a comma over his gray eyes. A black leather vest barely covered his massive chest, and he also wore green fatigue pants, combat boots, and a pair of Bowie knives strapped about his slim middle. He gazed at the fish suspended from the end of Ringo's line, noting the hole caused by one of Hickok's slugs, and saw entrails hanging from the cavity. "Is this a new techique for gutting a fish?"

"I was target-practicing and accidentally hit the fish," Hickok said.

The giant glanced at the gunman. "You've never accidentally hit anything in your life."

Hickok shrugged. "It happens."

"Are you taking my daddy away from the Home again?" Ringo asked.

"Nope," Blade replied. "I just came over to shoot the breeze."

"Good. Mommy said the next time you take him away without giving her warning, she's going to kick your butt."

Blade smiled. "She did, did she?"

"Yep," Ringo replied, nodding.

"She'll have to wait her turn," Blade stated. "My wife has first dibs on kicking my butt."

"Gee. Does Aunt Jenny pick on you like my mom picks on my dad?"

"Your mother doesn't pick on me," Hockok interjected. "We just have a squabble every now and then when she can't see the wisdom of my ways."

Ringo stared at his father in evident confusion. "Do you squibble because Mommy usually knows best?"

Geronimo cackled.

"The word is squabble," Hickok said, correcting his offspring. "And your mom doesn't always know best. I'm right some of the time."

"When, Dad?"

The gunman stared off into the distance, pondering.

"When?" Ringo persisted.

"I'm thinkin'."

Geronimo continued to cackle.

"What's so funny?" Ringo inquired.

"Ignore him," Hickok said. "He has a corncob stuck up his butt."

Ringo's mouth dropped open and he gawked at Geronimo's posterior. "He *does*? Doesn't that hurt?"

The gunman sighed and shook his head sadly. "Forget I even brought the subject up."

"How did he get it up there?"

"Drop the subject," Hickok said, and glanced at the fishing pole. "Why don't you go show the fish you've caught to your mom.''

''But shouldn't we take Uncle Geronimo to the Healers?'' Ringo asked earnestly.

''Geronimo is just fine.''

''With a corncob up his butt?''

''That's a figure of speech,'' Hickok explained.

''A what?''

''Never mind. Now go show the fish to your mom.''

Ringo frowned and walked to the southwest. ''Boy, you never tell me a thing,'' he mumbled.

''I heard that. I'll fill you in on figures of speech later,'' Hickok promised.

''That's okay. I'll ask mom how Uncle Geronimo got the corncob up there,'' Ringo said.

''No, don't bother your mother,'' Hickok said hastily.

''Why not?''

''She's busy doing housework, and you know how crabby she can get when she's cleanin'.''

''Mom's never crabby. But I'll let her know you think she is,'' Ringo proposed.

''No!''

''See you later,'' Ringo said, and gave a cheery little wave. The fishing pole over his left shoulder, he strolled toward the row of cabins situated in the middle of the 30-acre compound.

''Uh-oh. I'm in deep doo-doo,'' Hickok commented.

''You're always in deep doo-doo,'' Blade concurred.

''I don't know why these things happen to me all the time,'' Hickok said.

Geronimo, whose fit of mirth was beginning to subside, snorted and pointed at the gunfighter. ''I do.''

''Oh, yeah? Then why am I always stickin' my foot in my mouth?''

''Because you're an idiot.''

''Says you, you mangy cuss.''

The giant cleared his throat. ''Are you two through?''

''What do you need, pard?'' Hickok asked.

''I want to talk about Achilles.''

Geronimo abruptly sobered. "Him again?"

The gunman rolled his eyes and sat down on the bank. "Boy, when it rains, it pours."

CHAPTER TWO

Blade folded his steely arms across his huge chest and glanced from the gunfighter to the Blackfoot, the two best friends he had. "I didn't expect you guys to react this way."

"What do you want me to do? Leap for joy?" Hickok quipped.

"Haven't we discussed the subject enough already?" Geronimo responded.

"This is a man's life we're talking about here," Blade noted. "His future is at stake. How can you dismiss him so lightly?"

"Easy as pie," Hickok said.

Geronimo turned and gazed out over the survivalist retreat. "We're not dismissing him. It's just that we think you're making a mistake if you nominate Achilles to be a Warrior."

"Why?" Blade asked.

"We've been all through this, pard," Hickok declared. "That uppity upstart doesn't have the right temperament to be a Warrior. He's too cocky for his own good."

"Cockier than you?"

"Me? I'm as humble as they come."

"Yeah. Right. And cows fly," Blade said.

"Hickok's right," Geronimo interjected, then did a double take. "I don't believe I just said that."

"I am?" the gunman responded, and beamed.

Blade sighed. "Everybody and their grandmother seems to be dead set against Achilles becoming a Warrior. Plato doesn't like the idea. You two are opposed. Even Rikki-Tikki-Tavi took me aside last night to express his reservations."

"Rikki too?" Geronimo said. "He's one of the more level-headed Warriors. What more proof do you need that your idea isn't so hot?"

"Achilles is the best man for the job," Blade insisted, and surveyed the compound, thinking of the vacancy in the ranks of the Warriors, a vacancy that had to be filled as quickly as possible. He disliked having the Warriors undermanned. When there was a manpower shortage, the other Warriors had to make up the slack by pulling extra duty, and extra duty meant more rotating schedules, less sleep, and impaired effectiveness. As the head Warrior, he preferred to have the people under him performing at 100 percent of their capability at all times. With so many lives at stake, he could affort to demand nothing less than their very best.

Over 100 persons now resided at the compound that had been constructed by a wealthy survivalist named Kurt Carpenter shortly before the war. Carpenter had called his retreat the Home, and gathered together selected friends into a close-knit group he called the Family. For over a century the Family had lasted, despite the threats of madmen, scavengers, mutations, androids, drug lords, and others.

Carpenter, now referred to as the Founder by the Family members, had spared no expense with his considerable fortune in having the compound built. Predicting that civilization would crumble after the war, and foreseeing that his followers and their descendents would need to cope with a world driven insane by the devastating Armageddon, a world where barbarism would rule and law and order would no longer exist, Carpenter had constructed a veritable fortress. Sturdy brick walls, 20 feet high and topped with barbed wire, enclosed the site. Along the inside of each wall a deep trench had been dug, and using aqueducts, a stream had been diverted into the compound, entering under the northwest corner and exiting to the southwest. This inner moat was their second line of defense in case of a major assualt by enemy forces.

In order that the Family would be adequately protected, the Founder had created the Warrior class. Divided into fighting arms designated Triads, there were currently 17 men, woman, and hybrids who had taken the Warrior Oath of Loyalty. One of their number had recently died, leaving Zulu Triad one man short.

"Do you really think the Elders will go along with your recommendation?" Geronimo inquired.

"They will if I can find someone to co-sponsor Achilles with me," Blade said.

"Are you fixin' to ask one of us?" Hickok queried.

"I was hoping one of you would make the offer on your own initiative," Blade replied, and was discouraged by the silence that greeted his remark. Candidates for Warrior status had to pass through an ordained selection process. First, an active-duty Warrior had to agree to act as a sponsor. Usually only one sponsor was required, although there had been instances in the past where more than one active-duty Warrior had sponsored the same candidate. Once a candidate acquired a sponsor, then Blade would submit the candidate's name to the Family Leader, Plato and the rest of the Elders. After carefully reviewing the candidate's qualifications, the Elders would decree whether the candidate was acceptable or not. And if the hearsay getting back to Blade was true, Achilles might well be rejected.

Am I making a mistake? Blade asked himself. True, Achilles had attained a black belt in karate, but prowess in the martial arts was only one of the prerequisites for the post. It was also true that Achilles had qualified as an outstanding marksman, but marksmanship by itself meant very little. Where choosing a Warrior was concerned, personality and temperament were most important.

"Achilles will have to prove himself to me before I'll agree to co-sponsor him," Geronimo said.

"There isn't any way that peacock can prove himself to my liking," Hickok added. "He thinks he knows the answer to everything."

Geronimo glanced at the gunman. "Just like someone else I know."

"Like who?"

Blade cleared his throat. "What if Achilles *could* prove himself to your satisfaction? Would you vouch for him then?"

"How's he going to accomplish that miracle?" Geronimo quipped.

"If he does my dirty laundry for a month, I might reconsider," Hickok said.

"I thought Sherry washes your dirty clothes," Geronimo mentioned.

"She does. But the way I figure it, the less time she has to spend doing laundry and such, the more time she has to spend cuddling with her favorite hunk."

Blade took a step toward them. "You haven't answered my question."

The gunman shrugged. "Sure, pard. If you can figure a way for Achilles to prove himself to me, I'll vouch for the yahoo."

"The what?" Geronimo asked.

"A yahoo. If you had smarts like me, you'd know what the dickens a yahoo is."

"I know what a yo-yo is. I work with one every day."

"Quit callin' Blade names. You know how touchy the big guy gets."

"Why do I bother," Blade mumbled. He pivoted and headed for the enormous concrete blocks due south of their position.

Kurt Carpenter had divided the compound into thirds. The eastern section was maintained in its natural state or devoted to agricultural pursuits. In the center of the Home, arranged in a row from north to south, were the log cabins for the married Family members. The western section contained six immense bunkers, each devoted to a specific purpose. They were aligned in a triangular formation. Farthest south stood A Block, the Family armory. One hundred yards to the northwest of the armory was B Block, the sleeping quarters for single members. C Block, another hundred yards to the northwest, served as the infirmary. Due east of C Block a hundred yards was the Family's carpentry shop and general-purpose construction facility, D Block. Located at the northeast apex of the triangle sat E Block, the library Carpenter had personally stocked with hundreds of thousands of books. And finally, 100 yards to the southwest, was F Block, the building utilized by the Tillers for storing their farming equipment, and also for preparing and preserving food.

"See what I mean about touchy?" Hickok said to Geronimo, and hurried after the giant. "Hey, pard. Wait for us."

"Why should I?"

"Because we're your best buddies."

"Don't remind me," Blade said. "With buddies like you, who needs enemies?" He rested his hands on the hilts of his Bowies as he walked toward C Block, smiling and nodding at Family members he passed en route. The western third of the Home, particularly the wide track between the blocks, was where the Family congregated to socialize. Musicians sang or played their instruments, children laughed and played, and adults engaged in pleasant conversation. The weekly worship services were also conducted there, and most Family meetings, when the weather permitted, were also held outdoors between the blocks.

Hickok and Geronimo caught up with their friend, walking on his left.

"What's eatin' you, pard?" the gunman inquired.

"Nothing."

"You can't fool me. I know something is bothering you."

"Maybe I'm ticked off because no one seems to think I

know what I'm doing," Blade stated.

"Who said that? I'll personally shoot their toes off."

"You did."

Hickok almost tripped over his own feet. "I did? I never said no such thing."

"Neither of you believe Achilles would make a competent Warrior," Blade pointed out.

"So?"

"So I do. And by disagreeing, you're implying that I don't know what I'm doing."

The gunman and Geronimo exchanged glances.

"You're blowin' this thing out of all proportion. Just because we disagree with you doesn't mean we think you're a cow chip."

"It's the same thing, Nathan."

"It is not," Hickok responded defensively.

"Perhaps the real reason you're upset is because *everyone* feels the same way we do," Geronimo noted. "Maybe you're just taking your frustration out on us."

"Yeah. Not nice," Hickok declared.

Blade looked at them. "Haven't I done a fair job as the top Warrior?"

"You're the best Warrior the Family has had in its entire history," Geronimo answered.

"He can't draw a six-shooter worth spit," Hickok commented.

"Well, if I'm halfway proficient, then why is everyone doubting my judgment when I say that Achilles will make a damn good Warrior?" Blade snapped.

"It's not that we have anything against you," Hickok said. "It's just that Achillels rubs practically everyone the wrong way."

"Yeah," Geronimo agreed. "He's too . . ." he began, then abruptly stopped and cocked his head.

"What is it, pard?" Hickok inquired.

Geronimo gazed to the west. "Don't you hear it?"

An instant later everyone in the compound heard the sound, a rumble resembling distant thunder. The rumble grew in volume dramatically, and in seconds became a deafening roar as a gleaming, silvery jet streaked over the Home, flashing past almost at treetop level, seeming to shake the very ground with the din from its passage. Banking to the north, the jet arced high into the sky and began to execute a wide loop.

"It's the Hurricane," Geronimo said absently.

"What the blazes is it doing here now?" Hickok asked. "I thought the regular courier run wasn't until the day after tomorrow."

"That's the schedule," Blade said, watching the technological marvel swing toward the Home and thinking of all the times he had ridden in the aircraft.

The Hurricane belonged to the Free State of California, an ally of the Family's. Together they were but two of the seven factions comprising the Freedom Federation, an alliance formed when the leaders of the seven groups had signed a mutual self-defense treaty, resulting in a loose confederation of disparate members. California was one of the few states to retain its administrative integrity after the war, and due to the state's abundant resources had been able to preserve a level of culture similar to the prewar society.

Other members of the Federation included the Flathead Indians, who now controlled the former state of Montana, and the Cavalry, superb horsemen who ruled the Dakota Territory. There were also the Moles, inhabitants of an underground city located in north-central Minnesota, and a group known as the Clan. Refugees from the Twin Cities, the Clan had intentionally resettled in the small town of Halma in northwestern Minnesota, not far from the Home, so they could be close to the Family.

The seventh Federation member was the Civilized Zone, an area embracing the former states of Kansas, Nebraska, Colorado, Wyoming, New Mexico, and Oklahoma and part of Arizona and the northern half of Texas. The U.S. government had evacuated thousands of its citizens into the region during the war, and later, when the government collapsed, a dictator had seized power and renamed his dominion. Six years ago a descendant of the dictator had attempted to reclaim America as his own and been defeated, killed by Blade.

"I wonder why the Hurricane is here early," Geronimo said.

"Your guess is as good as mine," Blade responded, his lips compressing. A monthly courier service had been established, using the jets to carry correspondence and passengers from one Federation faction to the next. Because of the vast distances between them, the only means the Federation members had of keeping in regular contact was through the Hurricanes. The pilots normally stuck to their assigned schedules like clockwork, and whenever they deviated from their route there had to be an excellent reason.

It usually meant trouble.

Hickok glanced at the giant. "Maybe they need you to take the Force on a mission."

"I hope not," Blade said. "I'm not slated to return to California for another week and a half."

The Freedom Force—or simply the Force, as most referred to the unit—was an elite tactical team formed by the Federation leaders to deal with any and all threats to Federation security. Composed of a volunteer from each faction, the Force could be dispatched on a moment's notice to any point on the continent. Blade had agreed to serve as the head of the Force, and he alternated his time between the Home and the Force headquarters near Los Angeles. Recently he had adjusted his schedule so that he spent two weeks out of each month at the Home and two in L.A. Eventually he hoped to reduce his Force work load to where he would only need to stay a week in California every month. He intensely disliked being away from his wife and son, and now, as he saw the Hurricane dropping in altitude, coming in for a landing, he clenched his brawny fists and scowled.

This could only mean one thing.

He was about to put his life on the line again.

CHAPTER THREE

The Hurricanes possessed vertical-takeoff-or-landing capability, enabling them to ascend or descend much like a helicopter. Instead of the traditional lengthy runway required by most planes, they needed only 80 square feet of space from which to take off or land. As the pilot neared the west side of the Home, he put the aircraft into the VTOL mode and hovered over the field bordering the brick wall. As a security precaution, the Family kept the ground cleared for 150 yards in all directions from the compound.

An arrival of a Hurricane was always a fascinating event for the Family members. They flocked to the ramparts or streamed across the drawbridge situated in the center of the west wall, eager for a glimpse of the mighty jet, the only functional aircraft the majority of them had ever seen.

Blade, Hickok, and Geronimo joined the crowd moving across the drawbridge, with the giant in the lead.

"Hey, pard," Hickok said. "If the Federation bigwigs have another assignment for you, why don't you take us along instead of flyin' all the way back to Los Angeles? Geronimo and I can use the exercise."

"Speak for yourself, ding-a-ling," Geronimo retorted. "I'm not addicted to action like you are."

"Who says?"

"Face facts. You can't get by without your daily adrenaline rush."

The gunman snorted. "That's not true and you know it."

"Well, *excuse* me. Your weekly adrenaline rush, then," Geronimo amended, grinning.

"I hope there isn't another assignment," Blade reiterated.

"If there is, you can always take Achilles," Geronimo joked.

The idle suggestion prompted the giant to blink a few times, then smile. He threaded his way through the gathering throng, taking long strides, repeatedly saying, "Excuse me."

Its engines whining, the Hurricane slowly lowered to the turf 40 yards from the drawbridge, its nose pointed at the Home.

"Blade! Over here!" called out a friendly voice.

The Warrior spotted the speaker, an elderly man with kindly blue eyes and a long gray beard who was wearing a brown shirt and faded jeans. "Plato," he said in greeting, and walked over to the Leader of the Family. "Any idea why the Hurricane is here ahead of schedule?"

"None whatsoever," Plato replied, eyeing the aircraft. "This is most unusual."

Blade stared at the cockpit. The Hurricanes were designed to transport up to five passengers, and he could see two or three others seated behind the pilot.

Moments later the engines were shut down. The canopy slid back and a familiar face smiled at the giant and waved. "Yo, Blade! How goes it?"

"Fine, Pete," Blade replied.

"Captain Laslo seems to thoroughly enjoy his work," Plato commented.

"He does," Blade confirmed. "The man loves to fly."

Laslo lowered a green rope ladder from the cockpit and climbed down. "I've brought some guests," he announced, turning to the crowd and motioning upward.

Two people appeared, a woman and a man, both Indians, both attired in finely crafted buckskins. They immediately began to clamber down.

"Isn't that Star?" Plato inquired in surprise.

"It sure is," Blade said, wondering what had brought the leader of the Flathead Indians to the Home again.

Nineteen-year-old Star was following in her respected father's footsteps. He had been the previous Chief, and he'd perished in battle while opposing the forces of the dictator who'd previously ruled the Civilized Zone. The rest of the Flatheads had been defeated and compelled to work as slaves until they were eventually freed by Blade. In large measure because of her tireless efforts to reunite her tribe and inspire her people, the Flatheads later selected Star to be their new leader. Despite her youth, she projected a stately bearing and exhibited a maturity far beyond her years. Lovely black hair hung all the way to her waist, swaying as she came down the ladder. She reached the grass, turned, and scrutinized the assembled Family members, her dark eyes settling on the giant Warrior and Plato. She beamed and hurried over to them.

Blade smiled at her, his eyes straying to the other Flathead, a man in his mid-twenties whose features were a little too hard for Blade's liking. The man had black hair down to his wide shoulders, and he packed a pistol in a holster on his right hip and carried an M-16 slung over his left shoulder.

"Plato! Blade!" Star declared happily, walking up to the Family leader and giving Plato an affectionate hug before he had time to react. "Oh, I've missed you!"

"And I've missed you, child," Plato replied tenderly, embracing her gently.

A hearty laugh issued from Star's throat. "Child?" she repeated, and stepped back to take a good look at the man who had raised her for a while after the death of her father. "I don't think I qualify as a child anymore."

"You'll always be my little girl," Plato said softly.

Star glanced at the giant. "What do you think, Blade? Am I still a child?"

The Warrior chuckled. "I refuse to answer on the grounds my wife might overhear and beat me to a pulp."

"I don't mind answering," Hickok interjected. "I think you're a foxy momma." He straightened and scanned the crowd, then added, even louder, "Of course, you're not as foxy as my missus. No one is."

"Coward," Geronimo muttered.

"To what do we owe the honor of your visit?" Plato asked.

Star looked at Blade. "We need your help."

The Flathead bearing the M-16 had halted behind her and was regarding the Warriors rather coldly. Now he arrogantly stated, "No, we don't."

Blade faced the Warrior. "And who might you be?"

"I'm Iron Wolf, War Chief of the Flatheads," the man declared proudly.

"War Chief?" Blade gazed at Star. "I thought *you* were the Chief of the Flatheads?"

"She is the Principal Chief, but *I* am War Chief," Iron Wolf emphasized.

The giant locked his eyes on the Flathead's. "I wasn't speaking to you."

Iron Wolf bristled, his mouth curling downward and his eyes narrowing. For a moment he appeared ready to hurl himself at the giant, but a quick movement on Blade's left drew his attention to the gunfighter, the one called Hickok. The blond man stood with his hands on the pearl handles of his Pythons and a gleam in his blue eyes. Iron Wolf forced himself to relax, recalling the many stories he had heard about the man in the buckskins, and mustered a grin. "I didn't mean to offend you. My people have selected me as their War Chief, and I must be true to their best interests."

Star pivoted. "And *I* don't have their best interests at heart?"

"We don't need these outsiders to help us," Iron Wolf said.

"These outsiders are our friends."

"Friends do not butt in where they are not wanted."

"I want them to help us, and so do most of the other leaders of our tribe,'' Star remarked testily.

"Which is why I have bowed to the will of my people,'' Iron Wolf said humbly.

Hickok snickered.

"What is this all about?'' Plato inquired. "Why are you here?''

Star nodded toward the drawbridge. "Can we talk inside?''

"Certainly,'' Plato said, and took her hand. They walked off, Iron Wolf following, and Plato looked back at the giant. "Coming, Blade?''

"Be right with you,'' the Warrior replied.

"I don't trust that varmint,'' Hickok said softly.

"Nor do I,'' Geronimo agreed.

"So that makes it unanimous,'' Blade stated. "Geronimo, I want you to take care of Peter. See if he'd like some food. Hickok and I will get to the bottom of this.''

"Save a piece of Iron Wolf for me,'' Geronimo said. He headed toward the pilot, who was busy inspecting the underside of the Hurricane.

"Are you thinkin' what I'm thinkin'?'' Hickok asked Blade as they hastened after Plato and their visitors.

"I think Star is in more trouble than she realizes. Did you notice the tone he used when he referred to the Flatheads as *his* people?''

"I sure did.''

"Star could have a power monger on her hands.''

"She's a bright gal. She must know he's pond scum.''

"Maybe. But I'll have a talk with her the first chance I get,'' Blade said. They caught up with Plato and the others in time to overhear Star addressing the Family Leader.

"—held a council meeting of all the subchiefs and it was agreed that I should come see you. I persuaded Captain Laslo to fly us directly here instead of continuing on his normal rounds. He was supposed to fly to the Moles next, but he realized the importance of our mission once I explained everything to him.''

"The courier pilots are under standing orders to go where

they're needed," Plato mentioned. "They do an outstanding job."

"You'll get no argument from me," Star said. "The counselors didn't want me to make the journey alone, so it was decided that Iron Wolf would accompany me."

"Lucky you," Hickok quipped.

Plato glanced over his left shoulder. "Oh, there you are. Nathan, I'll thank you not to be rude to our guests."

"Wouldn't think of it, old-timer."

Iron Wolf made a show of studying the gunman from head to toe. "Although we haven't been introduced yet, I know you are the famous gunfighter, Hickok."

"I guess I am a mite well known."

"Yes," Iron Wolf said, and smirked. "They say the only thing faster than your hands is your mouth."

Hickok abruptly halted, his hands hovering next to his Colts. "I take that as an insult, friend."

"Take it any way you want," Iron Wolf retorted, stopping.

The gunman's next words were tinged with menace. "Any time you reckon you're man enough, I'm ready."

"How about right now?"

"It's your funeral, cow chip."

"Enough!" Star snapped, glaring at the War Chief. "These are our friends!"

"They're your friends," Iron Wolf replied.

"And as for you, Nathan," Plato interjected, "I believe you're way out of line." He looked at Blade. "Don't you agree?"

The giant's countenance was inscrutable. "Hickok, why don't you go give Geronimo a hand?"

"Sure, pard," Hickok answered dutifully, his icy gaze still riveted on the Flathead. He wheeled abruptly and stalked off.

Star uttered a nervous, flighty laugh. "Where are my manners? Did I forget to introduce everyone? Iron Wolf, this is Plato, the man who took me in after my parents were killed and the tribe was taken captive," she said, indicating the Family Leader. "And this big guy is Blade, the top

Warrior.''

"Pleased to meet you," Plato stated, offering his right hand.

"I've heard a great deal about you," Iron Wolf remarked, shaking hands. "You helped Star through a very trying time.''

"My wife, Nadine, did most of the helping. She took Star under her wing and gave the princess all the love and sympathy she needed.''

"You're too modest," Star mentioned. "Both of you were there when I needed you.''

Plato smiled at her. "And we'll always be here should you need us.''

Iron Wolf glanced at the giant. "And I've heard a lot about you too. They say you are the deadliest man alive.''

"Not true," Blade said, and pointed at the retreating back of the Family's preeminent gunfighter. "There goes the deadliest man alive.''

"Oh, really?" Iron Wolf responded, smirking.

Blade nodded. "Really.''

The War Chief regarded the giant for a moment, then stared at the gunman. "What makes him so deadly?''

"Do you mean other than the fact that there isn't a person alive who can beat him on the draw? Well, for one thing, he has the perfect Warrior mentality. He has a warrior's soul. And he has the will.''

"The will?''

"The will to kill. Not all men and women can kill when it's required. Hickok, on the other hand, will kill anyone or anything, anytime, if it's required in the line of duty.''

"How can you say he has the perfect Warrior mentality when he becomes offended so easily?''

"We all have our little quirks," Blade said flatly.

Iron Wolf seemed to ponder the information for a few seconds. "Perhaps I should apologize to him.''

"I'll do it for you," Blade proposed.

"You'd do that for me?''

"Sure? Why not?''

Plato cleared his throat. "Now that we have *that* out of the way, why don't we go to my cabin and discuss the reason for your trip to the Home?"

"I can fill you in while we walk," Star said, and looped her arm around his.

The four of them headed eastward, crossing the drawbridge and moving toward the concrete blocks.

"Whatever has brought you here must be extremely urgent," Plato commented after a bit.

Blade, walking behind them, inadventently tensed when he heard Star's reply.

"You don't know the half of it. Members of our tribe have mysteriously disappeared. Hunters have been torn to pieces in the deep woods. And the search parties we've sent out have never returned." She paused. "I think we have a mutant problem."

CHAPTER FOUR

"Why do you suspect mutants?" Plato inquired.

"Because of the tracks and other factors," Star said and sighed. "I suppose I should start at the beginning so you can fully appreciate what we're up against." She paused. "It all began about two years ago. As you already know, our tribe is now in control of the area once known as the state of Montana. Most of the whites were evacuated by the government during the war, but the government didn't bother evacuating the Flatheads. I guess they figured we weren't worth the effort."

Blade listened attentively, surreptitiously observing Iron Wolf the whole time, taking his measure of the War Chief.

"The land was left to the Indians," Star went on. "There are other tribes living in the region, such as the Assiniboine, the Chippewa, the Cree, and the Crow. There are a few Blackfeet left too, although most of them went into Canada at the outset of that war. So the Flatheads are the most numerous, and we've become the dominant tribe."

"Your ancestors would be proud of your accomplishments," Plato said.

"Well, all this has a point. You see, about two years ago a terrible tragedy befell one of our settlements in western Montana. When the evacuations occurred during World War Three, many of the towns and communities became deserted, abandoned ghost towns. Our people have moved into some of the old towns. One of them, Medicine Springs, was located near the border with Idaho."

"Was?" Plato said.

"Two years ago there were over a dozen families living in Medicine Springs. They made their living by trapping and hunting. Once a month a trader from Missoula would take his wagon down to Medicine Springs to collect the pelts the trappers had caught and to trade with the families," Star related, her visage downcast. "One day the trader arrived in Medicine Springs on his usual rounds and found everyone gone. Missing. Without a trace. Every man, woman, and child had just vanished."

The Leader's brow knit. "How could everyone simply vanish?"

"We had no idea. Warriors were dispatched to investigate the disappearances. Iron Wolf led the search party."

Plato looked at the War Chief. "What did you find?"

"Nothing," the Flathead said, his facial muscles tightening. "We looked and looked for weeks. We found where pots of food had been cooking on the stove, as if the people were interrupted while preparing a meal. We found nearly every pet, every dog and cat and goat, had been killed, torn to pieces. But we found no trace of the residents. Nothing. We scoured the forest for miles in all directions and didn't even find a footprint."

"How bizarre," Plato said.

"It gets weirder," Star informed him. "Medicine Springs was just the first settlement to be hit. Over the next several months the communities of Jackson and Grant suffered the same fate."

"And again we found nothing," Iron Wolf mentioned. "Almost nothing, anyway. A few strange hairs were discovered."

"Why were the hairs strange?"

"Because no one could identify them. My people are familiar with every type of animal known in our region. After all, we've fished, hunted, and trapped the Northwest for centuries. And yet no one knew what kind of hairs were found stuck to a broken window in one of the homes. They resembled grizzly bear hairs, but they weren't the same," Iron Wolf said.

"That's when the rumors started," Star added.

"What rumors?" Plato questioned.

"A lone hunter claimed to have seen a group of . . . things. He reported these creatures walked like men, but they looked like bears. Combined with the strange hairs that were found, it was enough for rumors to make the rounds, rumors concerning evil Bear People who were murdering Flatheads in their sleep."

"Has anyone else seen the Bear People?"

"No. But later, when the community of Lakeview was hit, unusual tracks were found, tracks displaying bearish and human traits," Star said.

"I saw those tracks myself," Iron Wolf stated. "They were the most bizarre tracks I've ever laid eyes on. We found them along the shore of Lower Red Rock Lake."

"Hmmmm," Plato commented, scratching his beard. "Did you ever find footprints made by the missing people?"

"No."

"Which would indicate the victims were carried away from their homes by the creatures," Plato noted.

"That's our guess," Iron Wolf agreed.

"Was Lakeview the last community to fall prey to these creatures?"

"Yes," Star replied. "Lakeview was attacked back in June. Since then there has been no word of the Bear People—until two weeks ago, that is."

"What happened?" Plato inquired.

"Something unexpected. We had already detected a pattern in the attacks. They all took place near the Bitterroot Range, and each one was farther south than the one before it. We alerted every town and community in the region, but it did no good. When Lakeview was hit, we knew the creatures were moving eastward. We expected them to show up at the town of West Yellowstone or even Gardiner, but they never did.''

''What happened two weeks ago?''

''A Flathead by the name of Eagle Feather took his family on a trip into the region once known as Yellowstone National Park. His wife and boys were abducted, and he was able to get close enough to the abductors to determine they weren't exactly human. They tried to lure him into a trap and almost killed him in a rock slide, but he got away and returned to our territory for help,'' Star said.

Plato suddenly halted. ''Yellowstone National Park? But that's in the Civilized Zone.''

''Technically, although no one lives there now. Both our people and theirs go there occasionally on family outings or whatever. The geysers and hot springs are quite an attraction.''

''I can imagine,'' Plato said absently. ''But the critical information is that these creatures have now entered the Civilized Zone. If they continue to head to the east or the south they'll encounter more and more inhabited towns. There's no telling how many lives will be lost.''

''My sentiments exactly,'' Star declared. ''Which is why I came to see you. So long as the attacks took place within our boundaries, I was content to view this as a Flathead matter. I mentioned the trouble we were having to a few of the other leaders at the Federation summit in Anaheim a while back, but I saw no need to enlist their aid.'' She frowned. ''Perhaps I made a mistake in waiting so long. Now these creatures have entered the northwestern corner of the Civilized Zone. More than one Federation member is at risk. This is no longer just a Flathead affair.''

''You acted wisely by coming to see us,'' Plato said in praise.

"I would have been wiser to have come sooner. Now I must contact President Toland of the Civilized Zone and inform him. Captain Laslo will fly me directly to Denver from here."

"I still say our warriors will find the creatures and dispose of them," Iron Wolf said. "We've been able to eradicate mutations in the past with no great difficulty."

"But these Bear People do not impress me as being typical mutations," Plato pointed out. "Normal mutations are a fact of life in the postwar era, and everyone knows that genetically altered animals must be dealt with on a continual basis. Such typical mutations, however, do not attack settlements. They don't abduct the entire population of a town and vanish in the forest. In short, they're nothing more than deformed beasts of the wild." He idly tugged on his beard. "These new creatures are different. They're obviously endowed with a higher, devious intelligence. And they may be operating according to a master plan currently beyond our comprehension."

Iron Wolf shook his head. "They're simple mutations, nothing more."

Blade stared at the ground, depressed, knowing the course of action he must take. Plato was right. These creatures weren't your average mutations, and they had to be stopped before they reached the more heavily populated regions of the Civilized Zone. He thought about the three types of mutations he had encountered over the years and wondered if the Bear People might be a new kind.

The term *mutation* applied to any and all forms of genetic deviation, a word that required further defining when alluding to a specific type. Ordinary *mutants* were animals born with their genetic code scrambled, and their condition was attributed to the incalculable amounts of radiation unleashed during the war, radiation that had saturated the environment and produced animals with extra legs or eyes or some other quirky combination.

Another variety of mutation were those known as *mutates*.

These resulted from the chemical weapons employed during World War Three, and they were radically different from ordinary mutants. Once a mammal, reptile, or amphibian was infected, they transformed into bloodthirsty monstrosities possessing insatiable appetites. Their bodies would become covered with pus-filled, rank sores, and they would mindlessly attack any living thing they met.

The third and final category of mutation, so far as was known, were the *hybrids*. They were the genetically engineered beings created in test tubes. Prior to the holocaust, genetic engineering had been the rage among the top scientists in the developed countries. They'd competed with one another to develop new species or improve existing ones. Patents had even been granted and huge amounts of money had changed hands. A nefarious scientist called the Doktor had created a legion of hybrid assassins to do his bidding only a few decades ago, and some of those mutations were still alive.

As if the matter wasn't complicated enough, new strains had begun to appear, hybrids spawned when their human parents gave birth to hideous creatures after the mother or father had ingested a toxic substance, whether radioactive or chemical in nature, subsequently resulting in bizarre embryos endowed with bestial, almost alien traits.

So which were these Bear People? Blade wondered, and gazed at Star. "I wish you had informed us more fully about these creatures sooner. You're right. This is now a Federation matter, and as the head of the Force, and acting under the authority bestowed on me by all of the Federation leaders, I'll be taking charge of the hunt for the things."

"Now wait a minute," Iron Wolf began.

Blade spun toward the War Chief. "Pay attention because I'm only going to say this once. I've been empowered to deal with any threats to the Federation as I see fit, and these creatures, these Bear People, definitely qualify. I have a job to do, and I'm going to do it whether you agree or not. I don't care what you think. And if you give me any grief,

Star will be taking you back on a stretcher.''

Iron Wolf glowered and clenched his hands. "I won't tolerate such talk from any man."

"Oh?" Blade responded, and stepped to within an inch of the Flathead. "Don't do something you'll regret later."

Iron Wolf's lips twitched and his features contorted in a mask of anger. He was compelled to gaze straight up at the giant, a position he found extremely uncomfortable. If he made a move, he knew the Warrior would flatten him in an instant.

"Enough of this!" Star snapped, speaking to the War Chief. "We're guests here, remember? Why must you antagonize everyone you meet?"

"They started it," Iron Wolf said defiantly.

"I think both of you are behaving like petulant children," Plato interjected. "This petty hostility must cease."

"Fine by me," Blade said. "Just so Iron Wolf realizes that I'm now in charge of the search for the Bear People, and that what I say goes."

"Blade is right," Star confirmed. "He was granted unlimited authority by the Federation leaders. We must do as he wishes."

"If you say so," Iron Wolf said, backing up a few steps, his spiteful gaze still on the giant. "But I can't say as how I like it. No one should have authority over Flathead territory. If I'm ever picked as Principal Chief, I'll make that clear to the other Federation Leaders."

"You do that," Star said coldly. "But for right now, you must abide by my wishes and the treaty we signed. Is this clearly understood?"

"Of course," Iron Wolf replied.

Plato placed his right hand on Blade's arm. "I'd like to talk to you for a minute in private." He looked at Star. "If you'll excuse us?"

"Certainly."

The Family Leader walked to the south, the giant right beside him, and clasped his hands behind his thin back. He waited until they were out of earshot before turning to his protégé. "What was that all about?"

"He just rubbed me the wrong way," Blade answered.

"I know better. You never provoke anyone without a valid reason," Plato said, studying the Warrior's face. "I took you under my wing when your dad was killed, remember? I can safely assert that the only one who knows you better than I do is your wife. So what was that all about?"

Blade rested his hands on his Bowies. "I suspect Iron Wolf is a power monger."

Plato glanced at the War Chief, thinking of the edicts laid down by Kurt Carpenter against permitting power mongers to flourish in the Family. The Founder had considered power-mongering politicians to be the scourge of the prewar society and strictly outlawed their existence. If any man or woman displayed a tendency to lord it over other Family members, that person was to be cast out from the Home. "What makes you think so?"

"Little things."

"Be specific."

"The way he talks, the way he acts."

Plato snickered. "Do you call those specifics?"

"I'm serious. I suspect he intends to take control of the Flatheads from Star."

"Perhaps he does," Plato said. "Is that any of our business?"

Blade displayed surprise. "Of course it is. The Flatheads are our allies. If there's a power monger in their midst, we owe it to them to weed him out."

"Do we?"

"I don't follow you."

"You've rightfully pointed out that as head of the Force you have the right to deal with external threats to the security of the Federation as you see fit," Plato said. "But I would question whether you have the right to meddle in the internal affairs of each faction unless those affairs posed a threat to the Federation as a whole."

"Are you saying we should mind our own business?"

"What do you think?"

Blade looked at Star and Iron Wolf. "I think you're wrong. How can you stand by and do nothing when the woman you helped raise could be in jeopardy?"

"We don't know that she is. For all we know, Iron Wolf could simply have an attitude problem. He might be prejudiced, might be a bigot. But that's not ample justification for one to jump down his throat every time he opens his mouth."

The Warrior shook his head. "I can't believe I'm hearing you say this."

"And I'm beginning to wonder if your position as head of the Force hasn't gone to your head."

Blade did a double take.

"You must be careful not to overstep your bounds," Plato advised. "You must walk a tightrope of responsibility, with the safety of the Federation on one hand and the rights of each Federation member on the other. An unwarranted mistake, such as an unauthorized interference in the internal business of any member, could well endanger the very existence of the Federation."

The giant stared thoughtfully at his mentor. "I never gave that aspect of the Force position much consideration."

"Then it's time you did so." Plato smiled and nudged the giant. "Now let's rejoin our visitors. And please, for my sake, resist any temptation to pound Iron Wolf to a pulp. Extend the man the benefit of the doubt until you uncover concrete evidence that he's a power monger."

"I'll try," Blade pledged. "Just be thankful I'm not Hickok."

Plato laughed at the notion. "One Hickok per planet is quite enough, thank you."

The strolled slowly toward the Flatheads.

"You know what I have to do about the attacks, don't you?" Blade said.

"Yes."

"I'll be leaving within the hour. The sooner we reach Yellowstone, the better. Laslo will fly us there."

"Who will you take along?"

"Hickok and Geronimo," Blade replied, then grinned. "And two others."

"Yama and Rikki?"

"No. I was thinking of Achilles."

Plato abruptly halted and pivoted. "Achilles? He's not a Warrior."

"But he wants to become one. And the only way he'll ever be accepted is if he proves himself to everyone's satisfaction. I'd like to take him with me to give him the chance to do just that."

"This is a most unusual request," Plato said. "Only full-fledged Warriors have gone on runs in the past."

"Would you do me a favor?"

"Anything. You know that."

"Call an impromtu meeting of the Elders. Present my request and get their consent."

Plato absently stroked his mustache, reflecting. After half a minute he nodded. "Consider it done."

"Thanks."

They resumed walking and had gone five yards when Plato stopped again.

"Wait a minute. You said you wanted to take two others on this mission. Achilles and who else?"

"The last person you would ever expect."

"Is this a guessing game? Who is it? Lynx?"

"No."

"Helen again? After all the trouble she gave you the last time, I wouldn't expect you to take her along."

"It's not Helen."

"Then who?" Plato asked impatiently.

Blade stared at the Flathead War Chief and grinned. "Mr. Personality himself."

Plato gazed at Iron Wolf and shook his head. "Perhaps I was mistaken about knowing you very well."

"Why?"

"Because you're more of a glutton for punishment than I thought."

CHAPTER FIVE

"There goes our ticket home," Geronimo commented.

Blade gazed skyward at the Hurricane streaking to the east, a gleaming arrow in the azure sky, and hefted the Commando Arms Carbine in his left hand. "Pete will be back to pick us up at this exact spot in one week."

"I just hope we can get the job done by then," Hickok mentioned. "These Bear critters might not be easy to track down."

"Never fear, my fellow Warrior. We shall persevere and triumph because the Spirit is with us," declared the handsomely proportioned man to their left in his resonant voice.

"Whatever you say, Achilles," Hickok responded dryly.

Blade looked at the aspiring Warrior, hoping he had done the right thing in bringing the man along.

Before his Naming, before the formal ceremony all Family members went through at the age of 16 when they were permitted to pick whatever name they wanted as their very own—a ceremony instituted by the Founder in an effort to insure his descendants maintained a historical connection to

their past—Achilles had been known as James Cooper. He'd
chosen his new name because of his abiding passion for the
works of Homer, particularly *The Iliad,* a work he had read
from cover to cover 24 times, corresponding to once for
every year of his life.

Achilles stood six feet in height and possessed a muscular
physique. A golden halo of blond curls adorned his head,
and eyes the color of turquoise regarded the world at large
with frank fearlessness. In keeping with the Family tradition
of encouraging every man and woman to wear whatever
clothing they felt best expressed their individuality, Achilles
had prevailed on the Weavers to construct a special one-piece
garment for him, a knee-length black tunic girded at the waist
by a brown leather belt six inches wide. He wore heavy
sandals, except in the winter when he preferred moccasins.
The item of his apparel that drew the most attention was his
flowing red cloak, which fell almost to his ankles and
billowed in the wind from the northwest.

Attached to Achilles' belt on his right hip was the only
knife in the huge Family armory that could justifiably rival
Blade's Bowies in size and craftsmanship. Forged in the rain
forests of Brazil by native artisans and exported by the
Brazilian government at a substantial profit in the decades
before the war, such knives were known as Amazons. The
Amazon Achilles carried had a 16-inch blade and gave the
weapon the reach of a short sword. Its Stag Micarta handle
was virtually unbreakable. In addition to the knife, Achilles
carried a Mossberg Model 500 Bullpup, a futuristic slide-
action shotgun. A leather ammunition pouch hung under his
left arm, its thin strap slanted across his chest.

"So which way do we go from here?" Hickok asked.

Blade pointed to the northwest. Captain Laslo had
desposited the five of them in a large clearing on the west
side of the Absaroka Range, within several hundred yards
of the Lamar River. Blade reached behind his back, checking
that the extra magazines were properly attached to his belt,
and headed out, cradling the Commando. Of all the machine
guns in the armory, he liked the Commando the best.

Resembling the popular Thompsons used during the Roaring Twenties, the 45-caliber Commando sported a 90-shot magazine.

"I still don't understand why we landed at this spot," groused the fifth member of their team.

The giant glanced at the Flathead War Chief. "According to the information relayed to Star from the man whose family was abducted, the last confirmed attack took place at the north end of the Lamar Valley. If the Bear People are continuing to migrate to the southeast, as we suspect, then they will be heading this way. They might still be somewhere in this valley, and with any luck we'll run into them somewhere between here and the spot where Eagle Feather saw them."

"You hope," Iron Wolf said sullenly.

"If you have a better idea on how to intercept these creatures, I'm open to suggestions," Blade remarked.

"Your reasoning makes sense," Iron Wolf conceded, then stared suspiciously at the head Warrior. "Why did you want me to come along, anyway?"

"As I explained back at the Home, I decided that I didn't have the right to usurp total control of the hunt for the Bear People. You were right. This should be a joint mission. And since you were the only Flathead around at the time, you were the logical choice to accompany us," Blade explained. "Unless you would have rather we brought Star along."

"No. Of course not."

"Was Star planning to stay at the Home until we return?" Geronimo asked. His prized tomahawk was tucked under his belt on his left hip. In a shoulder holster under his right arm rode an Arminius .357 Magnum. He held an FNC Auto Rifle in his hands.

"No," Blade responded. "Laslo is going to pick her up and fly her to Denver. She'll consult with President Toland, and I have no doubt he'll dispatch a military unit to assist us."

"Toland is dependable," Geronimo concurred.

"We shouldn't be too hard for them to spot," Hickok cracked while inspecting the lever on his Navy Arms Henry, a rifle in 44-40 caliber.

"Why's that?" Geronimo asked.

"All they have to do is look for a walkin' red tent," the gunman said sarcastically.

Achilles looked at Hickok. "Do you mean me?"

"No, I mean Little Red Riding Hood."

"Why must you always make fun of my cloak?"

"Have you taken a gander in a mirror lately?"

"I'll have you know that red cloaks were worn by the bravest warriors in ancient Greece. The Spartans, for instance, wore their red cloaks proudly into battle. A red cloak is a symbol of courage and manliness," Achilles said condescendingly.

"For one thing, this isn't ancient Greece. For another, you look like a character from one of those comic books in the library," Hickok replied. "Captain Raspberry. That's what we should call you."

Geronimo laughed.

"At least *I* know how to coordinate a colorful wardrobe," Achilles said stiffly.

"Meanin' what?"

"Meaning that Geronimo and you apparently believe drab attire is the best attire."

Hickok glanced down at his buckskins. "There's nothin' drab about my clothes."

"Have *you* looked in a mirror lately? No one with excellent taste could possibly view your crude clothes as aesthetically exciting, with the possible exception of a buck in heat."

The gunman made a choking sound. "I think I've just been insulted."

Geronimo chuckled, his eyes twinkling. "A buck in heat!" he repeated, beaming.

"As for you," Achilles said to the Blackfoot, "you actually are a walking tent. Whenever someone looks at you, they experience an urge to go find their sleeping bag."

Hickok cackled. "Sleeping bag!"

"Excuse me," Blade said, halting and regarding the trio critically. "We *are* on a mission, in case you've forgotten. Let's try to keep the noise down to a low uproar."

"My apologies, Blade," Achilles responded. "We were simply indulging in the basic rite of male bonding."

"Male what?" Hickok asked.

"I think he said male bonding," Geronimo stated.

"What does he think we are? Glue?"

"That's enough," Blade declared. "Not another word unless it's in the line of duty."

"I'm impressed," Iron Wolf interjected.

"Oh?"

"Yes, indeed. The discipline instilled in your Warriors is truly remarkable," Iron Wolf said, and smirked.

Blade rolled his eyes and continued in the direction of the river. The mission was off to a rousing start, as usual. Maybe Plato was right about him being a glutton for punishment. As if dealing with the Bear People wasn't enough of a challenge, he had to keep his eyes on the Flathead War Chief and try to force Iron Wolf into revealing his true nature. At the same time he had to watch over Achilles and make certain the novice didn't commit a grave mistake. He also hoped that once Hickok and Geronimo got to know Achilles better, they wouldn't rate him as the pompous egotist he appeared to be.

Yes, sir.

Definitely should be a fun run.

Blade alertly scanned the vegetation on all sides, noting the presence of birds and small mammals such as squirrels and chipmunks. He spotted a large hawk high in the sky to the north. The setting seemed so tranquil, but he knew from hard experience how deceptive appearances could be. He patted his left rear pocket, verifying the maps he'd brought along were still there. Yellowstone National Park had been the largest National Park in the United States, and the maps would undoubtedly come in handy. He'd spent 15 minutes in the library before departing the Home and read about the Park in one of the encyclopedia volumes.

Occupying the northwest corner of Wyoming, Yellowstone had been the largest National Park, embracing over two million acres. Situated on a plateau 8,000 feet above sea level, the Park had been famous for its geysers and hot springs. The Snowy Mountains were on the north, the Tetons on the south, the Gallatin range lay on the west, and the Absarokas were on the east. According to the encyclopedia, wildlife had been abundant because hunting had been prohibited. The scenic attractions also included sparkling lakes and rivers, steep gorges and canyons, and beautiful waterfalls.

Blade wondered how much the Park had changed during the past century. If man hadn't intruded, he expected to find animals everywhere. As far as he knew, only a few Flatheads and occasional visitors from the Civilized Zone ventured into the region. He hoped there were none in the Park now, not with the mysterious Bear People on the rampage.

A narrow game trail materialized directly ahead, leading down to the Lamar River.

Blade took the point, his finger on the Commando's trigger, scrutinizing the undergrowth. He'd opted to travel light on this mission, and consequently none of them had brought backpacks. They would live off the land, hunting or fishing for their meals and erecting makeshift shelters at night.

The banks of the river were low and skirted in places with groves of cottonwood. Birds sang and flitted about in the trees. A fish leaped out of the water and splashed down again.

The Warrior smiled as he neared the river. He could readily understand the reason the Park had been so popular prior to the war. If Yellowstone wasn't so far from Minnesota, he'd be tempted to bring Jenny and Gabe there for an outing. Thinking about his wife and son filled him with sadness. They had not been pleased at his sudden departure. Jenny had protested that she'd like to receive more notice when he went "gallivanting off to save the world." Her tone had been laced with sarcasm.

Blade came to the bank and halted, peering at the different tracks in the soft earth along the water's edge. The Lamar River was one of the clearest he had ever laid eyes on, broad but not deep. He could see the bottom and spied a school of fish swimming to the north.

"This Park is a virtual paradise," Achilles commented.

"Because the whites have not poisoned it as they have so much of the earth," Iron Wolf said. "Your people destroy everything they touch."

"Don't go blamin' us for what our ancestors did," Hickok stated.

"Why shouldn't I?" the Flathead retorted. "It was your race who fought World War Three. It was your race that contaminated the environment and tainted the air we breathe and the water we drink." He gestured angrily at the Lamar River. "Even this river could have radioactive particles resting on its bottom, polluting the water in subtle ways."

"Boy, what a grump," Hickok quipped. "A little thing like a nuclear holocaust, and you hold a grudge against the white race for life, huh?"

"I make no secret of the fact I'm not fond of you whites."

"Good. Then you won't take it personal if I tell you that you're a first-class scuzz-bucket."

"Not at all," Iron Wolf said smugly.

Blade glanced at the Flathead, recalling Plato's words about Iron Wolf possibly being a bigot. How had his mentor known? Blade would have sworn that the War Chief was a power monger, but perhaps he had been wrong. Time would tell.

"Do you despise all whites?" Achilles asked the Flathead.

Iron Wolf nodded. "None of you are worth the air you breathe."

"Even a superb physical, mental, and spiritual specimen of manhood like myself?" Achilles asked in all seriousness.

Hickok slapped his left hand over his mouth and his shoulders began bouncing up and down.

"Especially a conceited fool such as you," Iron Wolf told Achilles.

"Most irrational. You can hardly fault us for the mistakes of our forebears. That would be the same as blaming you for the death of George Armstrong Custer."

"Ahhh. You know some history. Then you must know that Custer was typical of your race. He was a prejudiced moron."

"I beg to differ," Achilles said. "Custer was a competent soldier, nothing more or less. His loss at the Little Big Horn could be attributed to the fact that he had failed to cultivate his reasoning powers to their full potential."

Iron Wolf blinked twice, then looked at Geronimo. "What did he say?"

"You're asking me?" Geronimo responded. "The day I start to understand Achilles is the day they can pickle my brain for posterity."

Blade suddenly straightened and motioned for silence. "Do you hear something?" he asked, listening to a faint rumble emanating from the north.

"I hear it," Geronimo replied. "Whatever it is."

They all turned in the direction of the sound, which grew rapidly louder and louder, a continual heavy drumming, arising on the far side of a low knoll less than 70 yards from their position. A billowing dust cloud swirled into the air behind the knoll.

"What the blazes?" Hickok exclaimed, perplexed.

"It sounds like a herd of stampeding horses," Iron Wolf mentioned.

A tingle of recognition rippled through Blade and he took a stride toward the water, wondering if they could escape across the river. "No, not horses!" he cried.

And an instant later a tremendous horde of buffalo pounded over the crest of the knoll and made straight for them.

CHAPTER SIX

For several seconds the three Warriors, Achilles, and the Flathead were riveted to the spot by the appalling sight of hundreds of huge bison bearing down on them.

The onrushing mass of thundering brutes consisted of bulls, cows, and a few calves. The males were six feet high at the shoulders, the females somewhat smaller. They had shaggy manes and long, scraggily beards. Dark brown, with even darker manes of hair on their heads and shoulders, they could weigh up to 2000 pounds. Wicked ebony horns protruded from either side of their massive heads, with the spread of a yard from tapered point to tapered point.

"Across the river!" Blade ordered, and plunged into the water, ignoring the frigid sensation that engulfed his lower legs. He surged toward the opposite bank, moving sideways, watching the approaching buffalo.

Hickok, Geronimo, Achilles, and Iron Wolf followed the giant's example.

The herd of racing buffalo was keeping to the east side of the Lamar River, running in a line extending from near the water eastward for at least 100 yards. They crashed through the undergrowth in their path, crumpling the bushes and uprooting small trees with their violent passage. Some snorted and bellowed. Those nearest the river occasionally were forced almost to the edge of the bank by the press of speeding bodies.

"Move it!" Blade barked. They were still within eight feet of the east bank and the water had risen to their waists. He wanted to get farther before the bison came abreast of their position. If some of those buffalo should slip into the water—

Some did.

The herd was 20 feet away when three of the bison nearest the river were pushed into the water, unable to resist the inadvertent shoving of their comrades, overpowered by the crush of the horned legion. Two of the three were bulls. The cow immediately attempted to scramble onto the bank again, but the wall of bison repeatedly battered her back down. The pair of enormous bulls didn't bother to try and regain the bank. They simply lowered their heads and surged forward, directly at the five humans blocking their route.

"Look out!" Blade yelled, darting to the left. He was the farthest from the east bank and stood the best change of avoiding the buffaloes, but he halted the moment he perceived that the others would not be so lucky. He raised the Commando, intending to stop the bulls before the beasts could reach them, but he was already too late and couldn't fire for fear of hitting his friends.

Geronimo found himself the closest to the bulls. He snapped the FNC to his shoulder and sent a half-dozen rounds into the buffalo on the right, but the animal wasn't fazed in the least. And then they were almost upon him and he did the only thing he could think of under the circumstances. The bulls were running side by side, with a foot of space between their horns. He managed to take a step to the left, aligning his body so the buffaloes would pass on either side, and elevated his arms over his head, sucking in his gut to make himself as slim as he could, praying all the while that neither bull would hook him on those deadly points. He saw the twin heads sweep past him, and the buffalo on the left brushed against his buttocks. A heartbeat later they were past and he was in the clear.

But not his companions.

Hickok and Iron Wolf were both in the path of the bulls, the gunman on the left, the Flathead on the right. They had mere moments to react.

"No!" Iron Wolf cried, and frantically headed for the bank.

"Try this!" Hickok shouted, and fired the Henry twice.

Neither buffalo slowed. The bull on the right tilted its broad head and slashed in a vicious arc, its right horn catching the Flathead War Chief squarely in the chest. Iron Wolf screamed as he was impaled, his arms thrashing wildly. The buffalo flipped its head and sent the human sailing into the river.

Hickok was trying to get off a third shot when the second bull struck him. The buffalo whipped its bony forehead upward, striking the gunfighter with the force of a battering ram. Hickok catapulted head over heels through the air and came down within two feet of Blade.

Leaving only Achilles. He was in the path of the bull that had struck Hickok, and he brazenly stood his ground, disregarding the other buffalo entirely. His acute mind worked lightning fast. He knew he couldn't hope to avoid the beast, not if the bull stayed on its current course. But what if the brute deviated by even a couple of feet? So thinking, he gripped the left border of his red cloak and extended his left arm to the side, flapping the cloak as he did.

The bull took the bait. It swerved at the red object and butted with its forehead in the same manner as it would during the rutting season when contending with rival males for the right to mount a female.

Achilles felt the cloak sway as the buffalo charged by within inches of his body. Water splashed onto his face, on his eyes, and for a few seconds the world blurred. He stood stock still, though, until he was satisfied the bull had continued to the south, then wiped his right forearm across his eyes, restoring his vision, and rotated to the left with the intention of aiding Hickok.

Others were already there.

Blade and Geronimo were assisting the sputtering gunman in rising, each supporting Hickok under an arm. Amazingly, the gunfighter had retained his grip on the Henry.

"Is he okay?" Achilles inquired.

"I'm fine!" Hickok responded, then coughed and spat water.

Achilles glanced at the bank, where the herd was beginning to thin out, then hurried to the Flathead.

Floating on his stomach, his arms outspread, Iron Wolf wasn't moving. The water around him had been stained crimson. His M-16 was nowhere in evidence.

"Iron Wolf?" Achilles said, and reached out with his left hand. He gently rolled the War Chief over, and one look served to confirm the worst. A gaping cavity in the center of the Flathead's chest revealed the ruptured flesh and the punctured heart underneath. Blood still seeped from the hole.

"How is he?" Blade asked.

Achilles looked at the giant and shook his head.

Frowning, Blade watched the last few dozen buffaloes run to the south, and when the final straggler had gone by he nodded at Geronimo and together they conveyed Hickok toward the bank.

"I can do it myself," the gunman stated.

"Don't exert yourself until we've checked for broken bones," Blade said.

"You were lucky that bull didn't snag you on its horns," Geronimo mentioned.

Hickok glanced at Iron Wolf, his eyes on the crimson-rimmed cavity. "I reckon I was," he agreed softly.

"Should we bury him?" Geronimo queried.

"We'll dig a shallow grave," Blade replied. "Achilles, haul the body out of the water."

"Right away," the aspiring Warrior responded, and bent to grab the Flathead by the back of the War Chief's buckskin shirt.

"Another mission gets off to a flying start," Blade muttered. "I wish we could have saved him."

"I thought you took him for a power monger," Hickok remarked. "If he was, then good riddance."

"We don't know for sure that he was," Blade said. "He might have just been bigoted. By bringing him with us on this run, I'd hoped to uncover his true character, to learn whether he was a threat to Star. Now we'll never know."

They came to the bank and stepped from the river, dripping water.

"You know," Hickok stated as his friends lowered him to the ground, "I've probably read every Western in the Family Library, including all the history books on the Old West. I've read about buffaloes, all about how the Plains Indians used the buffalo for everything from food to clothing. And I read about how the buffalo hunters killed almost all of the bison off. I always wondered what it would be like to meet one of the contrary critters face to face." He paused. "Now I know."

Blade knelt. "How do you feel?"

The gunfighter stretched his back, then probed his right side, feeling his ribs. "I'm a mite banged up and sore as the dickens, but I don't think any bones are broken."

"Take it easy for a while."

"I'm fine, I tell you."

"That was an order," Blade said, and stood, gazing to the south at the vanishing herd. A cloud of dust hung in the air over the buffaloes, marking their location.

Achilles deposited the Flathead a few feet away. "How will his death affect the mission?"

"It won't," Blade answered. "We'll still search for the Bear People, or whatever they are, and make certain they never attack another settlement or town."

"All we have to do is live long enough to find them," Geronimo commented.

"Stay frosty," Blade continued. "Those bison were just the beginning. Yellowstone abounded in wildlife before the

war, and I'd guess that the animal populations have increased
since then. There undoubtedly are a lot of wolves, mountain
lions, and grizzly bears in this region."

"Grizzlies?" Hickok repeated. "I've heard they can be
nasty when they want to."

"Compared to the black bears we're accustomed to seeing
around the Home, grizzlies are gargantuan," Blade said. "So
everyone stay alert at all times."

Hickok rubbed his chest. "You don't have to tell me twice.
I took enough of a beating to last me a year."

"I'll start digging a grave," Achilles offered, and surveyed
the nearby brush for a suitable limb he could use. He spotted
a broken limb 40 feet away and went to retrieve it.

"Did you notice how Achilles avoided that bull?"
Geronimo asked.

"I saw him," Blade replied. "That took a lot of courage."

"He may be the most conceited person I've ever known,
but he has nerves of steel," Geronimo conceded.

"What did he do?" Hickok queried. "I didn't see it."

"You were busy doing your imitation of a fish," Geronimo
said, and grinned. "A pitiful imitation, I might add."

"You wouldn't think my little dip in the river was so funny
if that buffalo had walloped you."

"Those of us with half a brain know how to avoid a
rampaging buffalo."

"You've got that right," Hickok declared.

"What? That I know how to avoid a buffalo?"

"No. That you've got half a brain."

Blade squinted up at the sun. "We still have six hours of
daylight left. After we bury Iron Wolf we'll head north."

"When do you expect the Civilized Zone troopers to reach
us?" Geromino inquired.

"Not for three or four days, at least. Even longer if they
have to come all the way from Cheyenne. I doubt they'll
reach us in time to be of any help against the creatures we're
after."

"We can get the job done by ourselves. We don't need
them," Hickok said.

"Speak for yourself," Geronimo replied. "I'd like to have all the help I can get."

Achilles returned bearing the limb. "This should do nicely," he said, and set to work, using the thick, jagged end of the branch to scoop out the topsoil.

"Hey, Homer," Hickok said. "What did you do in the river when those buffaloes charged us?"

The man in black paused and straightened. "Homer wrote *The Iliad.* He wasn't a character in the book."

"Who cares? I want to know what you did in the river."

"Might I ask why?"

"I'm curious."

Achilles shrugged. "Very well. I used my red cloak to divert the bull away from me."

"Your cloak?"

"Yes. Perhaps you're familiar with the bullfighting once done in Spain, Mexico, and several Latin American countries. A special breed of fighting bull would be pitted against a matador armed only with a red cape and a sword. The matadors would use the cape to control the actions of the bull. I simply applied the same principle to the buffalo," Achilles detailed, and grinned. "Quite elementary, actually. You would have been better advised to dodge that bull instead of trying to shoot it. Buffaloes are notoriously hard to kill."

"Gee, thanks for the tip. I'll keep it in mind in case I'm ever caught in a bison stampede again," Hickok said wryly.

Achilles leaned down and resumed digging. "Any time, my friend."

"Why do I bother?" Hickok mumbled.

Blade walked over to the corpse and squatted. He unbuckled Iron Wolf's leather belt, intricately adorned with blue beads, and removed the belt and the holster. "Who wants this?" he inquired, and slid the pistol out. The War Chief had carried a Taurus Model PT 92, an auto-loading 9-mm Parabellum with a magazine capacity of 15 rounds. Iron Wolf had kept additional rounds in a pouch attached to the side of his belt.

"I don't," Hickok said. "Auto-loaders are for sissies."

"I have no need for it," Geronimo responded.

Blade looked at Achilles. "What about you?"

"You don't want it?"

"I prefer my Bowies for close-in work."

"I'll take it, then," Achilles said. He dropped the limb and took the belt. "An excellent weapon should never go to waste."

"Can we quote you?" Hickok quipped.

Achilles strapped the belt around his wait, lining up the holster on his left hip, the butt jutting forward. He practiced a reverse draw, his hand turned palm out, then replaced the Taurus and performed a cross draw, getting the feel of the handgun. Satisfied, he adjusted the shoulder sling on his Bullpup and renewed his grave excavation.

"There's one thing I don't understand," Hickok mentioned.

"Just one?" Geronimo said.

"Yeah, smarty. About those buffalo."

"What about them?" Blade asked.

"Well, those big bruisers were going flat out."

Geronimo snickered. "What was your first clue?"

"You didn't let me finish, turkey. Buffalo usually don't just up and stampede for the heck of it. They've got to have a reason."

"So?"

"So what spooked those critters?" the gunman wondered.

"I believe I know," Achilles announced. He had stopped digging and was gazing to the north.

The three Warriors glanced at him.

"You do?" Blade said.

"They did," Achilles stated, and pointed.

Blade stood and turned, his jaw muscles tightening, hefting the Commando.

Over a dozen riders were silhouetted on the knoll's crest, most of them men, all well armed, each regarding the Family members with open hostility.

Hickok pushed to his feet. "Where the blazes did those cow chips come from?"

"More to the point," Geronimo mentioned, "are they friendly?"

As if in answer to the Warrior's query, the riders suddenly galloped toward the river, yelling and whooping and waving their weapons.

CHAPTER SEVEN

"Hickok, warn them to keep their distance," Blade ordered.

"With pleasure, pard," the gunfighter replied, pressing the Henry to his right shoulder. He sighted on the large man riding in the middle of the group, a man wearing a brown fur hat, and squeezed the trigger slowly.

The riders were 60 yards away when the Henry boomed and the large man's hat went flying from his head. He held up his right arm and bellowed a command. The entire group hastily reined up.

"Nice shot," Blade said.

"Piece of cake."

Blade studied the riders, counting 14 in all. Most of them wore buckskins, although a few flannel and black leather garments were visible. Most of the clothing appeared to be in shabby, even tattered, condition. Their weapons were a mixture of rifles, shotguns, and revolvers. He spied one assault rifle.

"Would you like for me to interrogate them?" Achilles asked.

Hickok chuckled. "What are you aimin' to do? March right up to them and tell them to spill the beans or else?"

"A sound suggestion," Achilles stated.

"And what'll you do if they don't cooperate?"

"Kill them."

The gunfighter's eyes widened and an appreciative grin creased his countenance. "Really? There's hope for you after all."

"Thank you," Achilles said. "I think."

The large man, evidently the leader, gave his rifle to another man, then rode forward, keeping his hands where they could be seen.

"Cover me," Blade directed, and walked out to meet the rider. He covered 20 yards and halted, letting the larger man come to him.

Casting nervous glances at the threesome on the bank, the leader approached to within ten feet of the giant and stopped. He was a big man in his own right, over six and a half feet in height and weighing in the neighborhood of 250 pounds. Unkempt, oily black hair hung to his shoulders, and he had a grease-stained beard. Grime caked his face. His apparel consisted of filthy buckskins that must have been in their prime a decade ago. When he smiled down at the Warrior he revealed four of his front teeth were missing. "Howdy, mister," he said gruffly, his gaze straying to the Commando. "I'm not packing, if that's what you're worried about."

Blade grinned. "I'm not worried. If you tried anything, I'd never have to bother with shooting you."

"Why's that?" the leader asked.

The Warrior jerked his hand at his companions. "If you so much as blink funny, my friend in the buckskins will add a nostril to your forehead."

The man glanced at the gunfighter. "Was he the one who shot my hat off my head?"

"That's him."

"Damn. That was a new beaver hat."

"The next time you encounter strangers, don't act as if you're going to ride them down," Blade advised.

"Who are you, mister?"

"The name is Blade. I'm the head of the Freedom Force."

"The what?"

"You've never heard of the Force?"

"Can't say as I have," the leader said. "My name, by the way, is Harmon."

"Are you a citizen of the Civilized Zone?"

Harmon uttered a short, sharp laugh. "Yeah, I guess you could say that. I was born there, anyway."

"What are you doing in Yellowstone?"

"In what?"

"In this area," Blade elaborated. "This whole region was once known as Yellowstone National Park, back in the days when the United States existed."

"I don't know nothing about no Yellowstone or United States. I do know this area is about as remote as they come, and hardly anyone ever comes here," Harmon said, then smirked. "Oh, a few nature-lovers show up every now and then."

Blade studied the man for a moment, then gazed at the band, calculating probabilities. "You're scavengers," he declared.

Harmon tensed. "There's no need to be calling us names, mister. I rode down here friendly-like to talk to you, not be insulted."

The Warrior locked his eyes on Harmon's. "You're all scavengers, or worse," he reiterated. "You and those others make your living by raiding and stealing, and I'd be willing to bet that you're wanted by the Civilized Zone authorites, which is why you hide out in this remote region."

Harmon scowled. "You have a great imagination," he said coldly.

"I'm right on the mark and you know it," Blade asserted.

"All you're doing is guessing," Harmon snapped. "Where's your proof?"

The question gave Blade pause. As the leader of the Force he could deal with scavengers, wherever he found them, as he saw fit. Scavengers were the bane of the postwar era, human locusts who ravaged and plundered at will, destroying everyone and everything they met. Legally, he had the right to terminate any scavengers he found, and ordinarily he would have blasted Harmon from the saddle without compunction. But Plato's words came to mind, troubling him, creating uncharacteristic doubt: "You must be careful not to overstep your bounds." What if, by some fluke, he was wrong? What if Harmon and the band weren't scavengers?

Harmon made a snorting noise. "I didn't think so, mister. You don't have no proof. Which means you can't do a damn thing."

Feeling supremely frustrated, simmering inside and ready to explode, Blade slowly shook his head. "I guess not."

"Then you're not going to shoot me in the back while I'm returning to my friends?"

The Warrior's eyes narrowed. "I don't shoot my enemies in the back."

Harmon sneered and started to wheel his horse.

"Wait a minute," Blade said.

Twisting in the saddle and regarding the giant suspiciously, Harmon halted. "What is it?"

"Have you seen any mutants recently?"

"Mutants?" Harmon repeated quizzically. "We see mutants now and then. A few weeks ago we killed a two-headed black bear."

"No, I don't mean the usual kind of mutations. Have you come across anything really strange, seen any unusual tracks?"

"No. Why?"

"I have reason to believe there's a group of particularly vicious mutants somewhere in Yellowstone."

Harmon snickered. "If there are, and if we find them, you won't have to worry about them anymore. So long, mister. We've got some buffaloes to butcher." He swung around and galloped toward his band.

Annoyed at himself, Blade turned on his heels and headed for his waiting friends. He'd certainly handled *that* poorly!

How stupid could he be? He never should have made an accusation he couldn't prove. Now Harmon and those others would avoid the Warriors like the plague. Or would they? If Harmon's bunch truly were murderous scavengers, perhaps they'd try to kill the Warriors just for the weapons. Quality firearms and knives were scarce in most areas. Even the Civilized Zone and the Free State of California relied heavily on arms preserved since the war. In the Outlands, men's lives were of less value than a good gun. So maybe Harmon would get careless and try to take the weapons. He hoped so. He wanted to wipe that smug look off the bastard's ugly puss.

"What's the deal?" Hickok asked as Blade approached. "Who was that lowlife?"

"The gentleman's name was Harmon," Blade disclosed. He heard the drumming of hooves and turned to see the band riding over the low knoll. "I suspect that all of them are scavengers."

"They why didn't you blow the guy away? We would've taken care of the rest."

"I didn't have any proof."

"What sort of proof did you want? A signed confession?" Hickok responded.

"We can't go around shooting lowlifes without justification," Blade said.

"Since when?"

Achilles cleared his throat and addressed the gunfighter. "Why must you give everyone such a bad time? You're a highly trained Warrior. Can't you simply accept Blade's word and leave it go at that?"

"Nope," Hickok replied. "I'm the curious type. I like to know the reasons things are the way they are." He paused. "And who asked you, anyway?"

Geronimo nodded at the knoll. "What's our next move? Do we go after them?"

"No. We'll continue with the original plan. We'll stick to the river and travel north. Let's hope we get lucky," Blade said.

"If you can call runnin' into a bunch of killer mutants luck," Hickok joked.

After burying Iron Wolf they began their trek, staying close to the water. Geronimo took the point and Hickok brought up the rear. In less than a mile they came abreast of a wide plain off to their right. Lying here and there were buffalo carcasses, and Harmon and his band were busily skinning the beasts and removing the choicest meat.

"I've never tasted buffalo," Achilles commented conversationally.

"Neither have I," Blade said. "But I read somewhere that it's delicious." He saw Harmon and a few of the others glance in his direction, and Harmon flipped him the finger.

"That fellow has deplorable manners," Achilles noted.

"He'll get his eventually," Blade predicted.

The land along the river was essentially flat and the undergrowth light. They covered several miles without incident. Once they flushed seven mule deer from a thicket and twice they spied beaver.

"May I ask you a question?" Achilles inquired at one point.

"What is it?" Blade responded.

"How much flack are you receiving about your proposal to nominate me for Warrior status?"

"Who says I'm getting any flack?"

"I do have friends, you know. They tell me that practically everyone who counts is against the idea. Plato. Most of the Elders. Even all of the Warriors."

"I wouldn't say *all* of the Warriors are against the idea."

"Who isn't?"

Blade thought for a moment. "Lynx, for one."

"Oh. Him," Achilles said softly. "Yes, I know. He told me that he doesn't care if I'm selected or not, just so long as he can go on a mission sometime this millennium."

"Sounds like Lynx," Blade observed.

"You still haven't answered my question."

"As I informed you before we left, there is considerable opposition to the idea. I'm not about to lie to you. If you want to be a Warrior, you must first prove yourself to a lot of people.''

''To you?''

''You know better.''

Achilles stared at the giant. ''I appreciate the fact you're going to bat for me.''

''Everyone deserves a fair chance. You've been branded as arrogant and stuck-up by those who don't know you very well. They don't realize your so-called arrogance is really nothing more than a bad case of overconfidence.''

''How can a person have too much confidence?''

Blade gazed at a few dozen antelope munching contentedly on grass on the far side of the river. ''Self-assurance is one thing. But having so much confidence that you begin to think of yourself as perfect and infallible borders on vanity. While you don't necessarily view others as inferior, you do think of yourself as a superior person. And your attitude comes across as arrogance to other people.''

''I know,'' Achilles said, and sighed. ''It's not like I'm unaware of the effect I have on those around me. I'm not an idiot. With an I.Q. of one hundred and forty, I'm smarter than most—''

''There you go again,'' Blade interrupted, and grinned.

''See? I do it unconsciously,'' Achilles stated. ''No matter how hard I try to be humble, I can't. I simply state the facts, and it seems as if the word modest isn't in my vocabulary.''

''At least you're aware of the problem. Work on it. You might make a change for the better.''

''But can I perform this miracle in time to be picked as a Warrior?''

''I honestly don't know. Give it your best shot. I didn't peg you as a quitter.''

''Thanks. I mean it.''

They continued onward, attended by the buzzing of insects, the chirping of birds, the rustling of the trees by the mild breeze, and an occasional splash in the river as a fish leaped up out of the water. Forty yards ahead the river curved to the right, and the riverbank at that point was covered by a dense thicket, the bushes being over eight feet in height. A few willows were interspersed with the underbrush. The thicket extended for 30 yards to the east.

Geronimo, who was 40 feet in front of Blade, halted and looked back. "Should we go around it?"

"See if you can find a trail through it."

Nodding, Geronimo walked closer to the vegetation.

Achilles looked at the head Warrior. "I hope I'll be able to repay you someday."

"You can repay me by always discharging your duties properly if you're selected. That, and learning to behave like a normal human being."

"Like Hickok, for instance?"

They both laughed.

"I heard that!" the gunman declared from 12 feet behind them.

Blade grinned and idly gazed skyward. Flying to the west were four large white birds unlike any he had ever beheld. They were five feet long, with white feathers, broad wings, and big beaks a third the size of their bodies. Each had a yellow throat pouch. He watched them for a minute before he identified them from pictures he had once seen in a book in the library. They were pelicans. What in the world were pelicans doing in Yellowstone National Park? He'd always associated them with the sea. Did they nest on the many lakes in the Park?

"When we stop for the night, I'd like to volunteer for the first guard shift," Achilles offered.

"Trying to impress me?" Blade asked.

"No. I'd like to show Hickok and Geronimo that I'm just one of the guys. If I pull my weight on this assignment, they might change their opinions of me."

"That's what I'm counting on."

"But will it be enough to convince the Elders?"

"If Nathan, Geronimo, and I all make a special appeal to the Elders to have you instated, they'll have to present an irrefutable argument to reject you," Blade noted, gazing at Geronimo.

The stocky Warrior had reached the thicket and was searching for a way through. He moved to the right, then pivoted and smiled. "Here's a deer trail. Just what we need."

Blade had opened his mouth to acknowledge the information when behind his friend an immense, bulky form reared up in the thicket, its jaws wide, its five-inch claws glinting in the bright sunlight.

The awesome form of a grizzly bear.

CHAPTER EIGHT

Blade broke into a run, swinging the Commando barrel up. "Behind you!" he bellowed. "A grizzly!"

Reacting instinctively, not even bothering to glance at the thicket, Geronimo dived forward. He landed on his left shoulder and rolled onto his back, the FNC stock pressed against his thigh, the assault rifle at a slant.

Uttering a rumbling growl, the grizzly dropped onto all fours and barreled from the undergrowth, going for the human in green.

Geronimo fired from a range of only six feet, and he heard his rounds smacking into the bruin's wide skull. He saw the grizzly halt and swipe at its face, as if batting at bothersome mosquitoes, giving him the time he needed to leap to his feet and run.

The grizzly lumbered in pursuit.

"Out of the way!" Blade shouted, motioning with his right arm and angling to the left, trying for a clear shot.

Geronimo obliged by abruptly darting to the east.

Instantly Blade cut loose, squeezing the trigger and holding it down, feeling the Commando buck in his arms as he sent a hail of heavy slugs into the beast. He heard more gunshots to his right, the sharp retort of Hickok's Henry and the deeper discharge of Achilles' Bullpup.

A series of red dots blossomed on the grizzly's head, but instead of falling it charged, making straight for the giant human.

Blade kept firing, expecting the bear to go down long before it reached him. There wasn't an animal alive that could absorb 90 rounds from a machine gun and still keep coming. Or so he believed.

The grizzly never slowed. Fifteen hundred pounds of sinew and muscle, seven feet long and almost five feet high at the shoulders, with its bulging hump adding to its height, the bruin was virtually unstoppable unless pierced in the brain or the heart, and even then the beast's tremendous vitality could drive it onward.

The Commando went empty when the grizzly was still eight feet away, and Blade reversed his grip, taking hold of the gun by the barrel and sweeping the stock overhead, prepared to use the Carbine as a club. He could see the bear's slavering, yawning maw, and the animal's musculature rippling under its coat of brown fur. Grasping the barrel firmly, he waited until the very last second, until the grizzly was almost on top of him, and then swung with all of his strength, slamming the stock onto the bruin's head.

Not breaking its stride, acting as if it was impervious to the blow, the grizzly plowed into the human.

Blade felt a jarring impact in his abdomen and chest, and he was flung backwards. Something cut into his left shoulder, producing an intense stinging sensation. His arms flailing, short of breath and in exquisite pain, he tumbled onto his back. Above him loomed the bear, and he braced for the crunching of strong teeth on his body.

The grizzly reared its head and spread its mouth wide, about to bite, when unexpectedly the bear sprawled forward, venting a loud growl, collapsing onto its victim's legs.

Blade hurled the Commando aside and whipped his Bowies from their sheaths. For a moment, as the massive bear lay still with its eyes closed, its weight causing excruciating agony from his knees down, he thought the beast was dead. He bent toward it, intending to try and lift the bear's head and shoulders so he could slide his legs out.

The grizzly opened its eyes and fixed a baleful gaze on the Warrior, then began to rise.

Realizing the bruin could disembowel him with one slash of its sharp claws once it regained its footing, Blade took the offensive, deliberately learning forward at the waist, placing his face within inches of the bear's, and speared his gleaming Bowies into the bruin's eyes before the animal could snap at him.

A mammoth cry of rage issued from the grizzly and it jerked its body backwards:

Blade held onto the hilts of his knives and shoved erect the second his legs were free. The grizzly lashed wildly at him with its right forepaw, and he darted to the right to evade its claws.

Blood streaming from its sliced orbs, the bear shook its head and shuffled after the human.

Tensing his legs for a spring, Blade detected a motion out of the corner of his left eye.

Achilles and Hickok materialized, their weapons blasting at point-blank range. Four, five, six shots sounded, and with the sixth the grizzly bear grunted and fell, dead in its tracks, its head thudding onto the ground.

Hickok shot the bruin once more for good measure, then lowered the Henry. "I was beginning to think this critter would never go down," he commented in amazement.

"Had the brute not fallen when it did, I was prepared to dispatch it with my Amazon," Achilles said.

"Your toothpick against this dinosaur? Give me a break," Hickok quipped.

"Your comparison is in error," Achilles corrected him. "Dinosaurs were reptiles. This bear is a mammal."

"Really? How did we get by all these years without your wisdom?"

Blade listened inattentively to their exchange, breathing

deeply, restoring his composure. The grizzly attack had made
his adrenaline surge. He looked down at his Bowies and saw
the bear's blood dripping from both knives. Footsteps
sounded on his right.

"Are you okay?" Geronimo inquired.

"Fine," Blade replied softly.

"What about your shoulder?"

Blade recalled the stinging sensation and glanced at his left
shoulder. With a start he realized the grizzly had nailed him.
There were five deep gashes, each over an inch deep. The
bear's claws had torn through his leather vest and his flesh
as if both were made of putty, and blood flowed from all
five slits.

The gunfighter hastily stepped clower. "Damn!" he vented
a rare oath. "I didn't know the varmint had clipped you."

"You were too busy flapping your gums," Geronimo said,
and slung the FNC over his shoulder. He moved in front
of the gaint and motioned for Blade to sit. "Let me take a
look at it."

"They're only scratches," Blade said, and sat down on
a clump of grass. He wiped the Bowies clean on his pants
and replaced them in their sheaths, then removed his vest,
grimacing as he pulled the garment from his left shoulder.

Geronimo inspected the five gashes, gingerly probing with
the tips of his fingers. "We need to stop the blood flow.
Hickok, did you wear underwear on this trip?"

"Whether I'm wearin' my drawers or not is none of your
beeswax, pard."

"I couldn't care less about your flea-infested drawers,"
Geronimo said. "Did you wear a T-shirt? I didn't, and we
can usc one to staunch the blood."

"Oh," Hickok responded sheepishly. "No, darn it. I'm
not wearin' a blasted T-shirt."

"I am," Achilles declared. "I'll gladly remove it to help
Blade."

"Then quit jabberin' and get the blamed thing off," Hickok
prompted.

Achilles deposited the Bullpup at his feet and started to

take off his red cloak. He happened to gaze in the direction of the thicket and abruptly froze. "What in the . . ." he blurted.

The others glanced at the undergrowth.

"What did you see?" Blade asked, scouring the vegetation, speculating there might be another grizzly.

"I'm not sure," Achilles replied. "A hairy face of some sort. It was there one instant, gone the next."

"You were probably looking at Hickok and didn't know it," Geronimo cracked.

"Very funny, you mangy Injun."

Blade slowly stood. He saw his Commando lying nearby and quickly retrieved the weapon, then ejected the spent magazine and inserted a fresh one.

"Do you want me to go take a look?" Hickok volunteered.

"No," Blade responded. "We'll stick together. We've only been in Yellowstone a few hours, and already we've lost one man and come close to losing one or two others." He stared at Achilles. "Do you have any idea at all what you saw? Could it have been a bear?"

"I wish I could say," Achilles answered. "I saw dark hair and beady eyes and that was it."

"Okay. Hickok, you'll keep us covered. As soon as my wound is taken care of, we'll move on."

"You've got it," the gunfighter replied. He fed cartridges into the Henry and strolled a few yards to the north, eyeing the thicket. "If there's another grizzly in there, it's dead meat."

"Breath on it. That'll do the trick," Geronimo suggested.

Blade walked toward the river. The blood from the cuts had diminshed to a trickle and the pain in his chest and his legs had subsided. He was eager to get out of there and locate a defensible site for their camp. At the rate things were going, what with having to contend with buffaloes, scavengers, and a grizzly before the sun even set, they'd have to take every prudent precaution to make it through the night. At the edge of the river he knelt and splashed the cold water on the gashes, letting the liquid seep into each cut, goose bumps breaking out on his skin.

Geronimo ran up bearing a white T-shirt. "Here. Soak this and press it on the wound."

"Thanks," Blade said, and glanced over his right shoulder to see Achilles donning the black tunic. He took the T-shirt and submerged the fabric, holding it under to saturate the material. "It's a good thing we brought Achilles along instead of Helen," he mentioned, and grinned. "I'd look silly as all get out with a bra wrapped around my shoulder."

"Helen doesn't wear a bra."

Blade looked at his friend. "How would you know?"

"Hickok told me."

"And how would *he* know?"

"He claimed he overheard Helen and Sherry talking one day."

"They were discussing *bras*?"

Geronimo snickered. "It seems that Sherry was complaining about the fact that it takes Hickok about an hour to remove her bra on their whoopee nights. She usually falls asleep by the time he figures out how to undo the clasp."

"Nathan admitted this to you?" Blade queried in disbelief.

"Well, actually, he came up to me and asked if I'd give him pointers on how to unfasten a bra. I had to pry the reason out of him."

"Did your pointers help?"

Geronimo beamed. "Now he takes two hours."

Blade chuckled and stared at the river, noticing the shallow depth, and then gazed at the opposite shore. A gently sloping hill approximately 100 yards to the west attracted his interest. The crown of the hill appeared to be flat and not more than two dozen yards in circumference. "Get Hickok and Achilles."

"Right away," Geronimo said, and hastened off.

Given the fact the mission had turned into a typical fiasco, and bearing in mind that he should rest his shoulder until the blood flow ceased, Blade decided to use the top of the hill as their campsite for the night. He'd hoped to proceed much farther north than they had, but he had to adapt to the circumstances. Continuing half-cocked would avail them nothing. He raised the T-shirt and dabbed tentatively at the cuts.

A small fish swam past him, not a yard away.

Blade studied the hill again. The setup appealed to him. The slopes were covered with grass, which would deny any adversaries cover for a clandestine attack. Beyond the hill lay a field dotted with trees and a few boulders. Granted, at night anyone with a modicum of skill would be able to creep close to the crown before being detected, but the terrain worked in the Warriors' favor. Having a field border their camp was preferable to stopping for the night in a forest.

"Here they are," Geronimo announced, returning with the gunman and Achilles. "And here's your vest," he said, and extended the black leather garment.

Blade took his vest in his left hand, slung the Commando over his right arm, and stood. "That hill will be where we stay tonight," he informed them. "We'll cross here."

"I'll take point," Hickok said, and waded into the river.

Achilles was adjusting his red cloak. "What about supper?"

"We'll hunt for game after we check out the hill," Blade stated, and followed the gunman. The water invigorated him, and he strode to the far side rapidly. Once on the bank he pivoted and scrutinized the thicket, but there was no sign of anyone or anything watching them. Good. They'd experienced enough grief for one day. He wheeled and headed for the hill.

Hickok was already 20 feet off.

A dull ache pervading his left shoulder, Blade thought of his wife and son and frowned. He missed them terribly, as usual, and he wondered if it would always be the same. For years he had been going on missions for the Family or the Force, and on each one he invariably pined to be with Jenny and Gabe. On each mission he felt gnawing guilt at being away from his loved ones, knowing how much they missed him and disliked his extended absences. He toyed with the notion of retiring from the Warrior ranks in a few years, after the major menaces to the safety of the Federation were eliminated.

Who was he kidding?

The list of Federation enemies seemed to be growing geometrically. There were the Soviets in the East, the Technics in Chicago, the Superiors in Houston, the New Order of Mutants in the Pacific Northwest, the Lords of Kismet in Asia, the Peers in Atlanta, the Gild of professional assassins, and others. He was deluding himself if he believed they could all be defeated within a few years. A few *decades* would be more accurate.

Engrossed in his contemplation, Blade hiked to within 50 feet of the hill. He held the cool, damp T-shirt against his shoulder the entire time. Possessing complete confidence in his fellow Warriors, believing they would spot any threat in time to warn him, he failed to exercise his customary vigilance, and he didn't realize he had made a mistake until several seconds later.

A shot rang out and a bullet struck the earth next to his left foot.

CHAPTER NINE

Blade dove to the right, unslinging the Commando as he did, releasing the T-shirt and vest, forgetting all about his shoulder. He landed on his elbows and knees and scanned the terrain ahead, seeking the sniper.

Hickok had already flattened. He twisted and pointed up at the top of the hill.

Training the Commando on the crown, Blade debated whether to charge up the slope. Whoever had fired that shot could easily have killed him. So the shot must have been meant as a warning. But who'd fired it? And why?

"You down there!" a man's voice called out. "You're not welcome here! Leave at once or the next time I won't miss!"

Hickok made a gesture, signifying he was ready to circle around the hill and sneak up on the man from the rear.

Blade shook his head. "Who are you? Why did you shoot? We mean you no harm."

"My name is unimportant," the man replied. "All you need know is that I'm a Flathead and I make my living by hunting and trapping, which means I can hit what I aim at.

Now leave!"

The Warrior rose to his knees. "If you're a Flathead, then you must know who I am," he yelled.

"I've never laid eyes on you before, white man."

"Have you heard of Blade?"

"The Warrior and the man who leads the Force? Are you claiming to be him?"

Blade rose to his full height. "I am."

"How do I know you speak the truth? Whites are notorious liars."

"If you've heard of me, then you probably know my description. Take a good look."

Silence descended.

Blade waited patiently for the Flathead to make the next move. He looked back at Achilles and Geronimo, both of whom were watching the hill anxiously. When he faced forward again, a man stood in plain view at the top of the hill.

"Your appearance matches the description I have heard of the Warrior named Blade, but how do I know you're truly him? How can I trust you?"

The giant smiled. "I'm not in the habit of lying to an ally of the Family. And Star would be quite upset if I blew away one of her people."

"Did Star send you?" the man asked, taking several strides down the slope. He wore buckskins and carried a Winchester.

"Yes," Blade revealed. "She flew to the Home and requested our assistance. We're searching for the creatures responsible for abducting the wife and sons of a tribesman of yours called Eagle Feather."

The Flathead suddenly broke into a run and sprinted down the hill at a reckless speed. He hardly glanced at Hickok when he passed the gunman, and drew to an abrupt halt a few yards from the giant. "I'm Eagle Feather!" he declared breathlessly.

Blade studied the Flathead, liking what he saw. The man's rugged features and frank brown eyes conveyed an impression of innate honesty and strength, tempered by the transparent anxiety he unconsciously radiated. "I thought you had returned to Flathead territory," Blade mentioned. He scooped up the vest and T-shirt.

"I did. I went to Gardiner and reported what had happened, and a messenger was immediately dispatched to inform Star. Then I returned to Yellowstone to hunt for my family," Eagle Feather related, sorrow deepening the lines in his face. "I haven't had any luck."

"Have you located the creatures?"

"No," Eagle Feather said. He glanced around as the giant's companions converged on him. "I apologize for firing at you. I assumed you were part of a scavenger party I've seen roaming this area."

"We've seen them too," Blade related, and gestured at his friends as he introduced them. "This is Hickok, Geronimo, and Achilles. They're also from the Home."

"Pleased to meet you," Eagle Feather told them. "Thank you for coming to help. If you only knew how much my wife and sons mean to me . . ." he said, and stopped, choking on the words.

Geronimo stepped forward and placed his hand on the Flathead's shoulder. "We won't rest until we've found them."

"Thank you," Eagle Feather said softly, then cleared his throat. "To which tribe do you belong?"

"I'm a Warrior. I live at the Home," Geronimo divulged. "My ancestors were Blackfeet."

Eagle Feather motioned toward the hill. "Please, join me. I've made camp at the top. A few hours ago I shot a buck, and I was in the process of butchering it when I heard shots and spotted you."

"I could go for some venison," Hickok said. "You're on, Eagle Tail."

"That's Eagle Feather."

"Whatever," Hickok said, and headed for the slope.

"Pay no attention to him," Geronimo advised the Flathead. "He suffered an unfortunate accident as a baby."

"He did?"

"Yes. Actually, he's a medical marvel. He's one of the

few people ever born without a brain."

"I heard that!" Hickok stated.

Eagle Feather glanced quizzically at Blade. "Are they friends?"

"The best," the giant confirmed. "They're like brothers. Think of them as matching bookends. Frick and Frack."

They walked westward, Achilles bringing up the rear.

"Are all four of you Warriors?" Eagle Feather inquired.

"Geronimo, Hickok, and I are," Blade replied. "Achilles will be soon, I hope."

"I've heard many stories about the Warriors. My tribe would still be languishing in bondage if you Warriors had not defeated Samuel the Second."

"We had a little help," Blade said.

"Speaking of help, why didn't other Flatheads return here with you?" Geronimo questioned. "Why did you come back alone?"

"They sent the word out to every man living within forty miles of Gardiner," Eagle Feather answered. "I was too impatient, too filled with worry, to wait for them to organize their rescue mission. So I left directions and came on ahead. I expect them to show up any day now."

"And there will be a military unit dispatched by the Civilized Zone arriving in a few days," Blade disclosed.

"Between all of us, we'll find your wife and sons," Geronimo added.

"I pray we will," Eagle Feather said. "Every day that goes by increases the odds they won't be found alive."

"Don't talk like that," Geronimo said. "Have faith."

"I have faith in the Spirit-in-All-Things, but the Spirit doesn't guide the footsteps of the Bear People. The Spirit can't gain entry to a closed mind."

"Haven't you seen any sign of the creatures?" Blade probed.

"A few tracks, and that's all. Whatever they are, they seem to move across the countryside like ghosts."

"They're flesh and blood, which means they can bleed,"

Geronimo said. "Once we catch up with them, we'll do the world a favor and eliminate them."

"It won't be easy," Eagle Feather stated. "Some of my people believe the Bear People are demons."

"Nonsense. They're mutations, plain and simple," Geronimo countered.

"I know. But the knowledge doesn't make my heart any lighter."

They ascended the slope in single file.

Blade felt enormous sympathy for the Flathead. He could readily imagine the emotional turmoil Eagle Feather must be going through. If the same thing had happened to Jenny and Gabe, he'd be frantic, out of his mind with apprehension. He resolved to do everything humanly possible to rescue Eagle Feather's wife and sons.

"Tonight the Bear People will be abroad," the Flathead mentioned.

Blade glanced over his left shoulder. "How do you know?"

"There will be a full moon."

"I don't get the connection."

"Didn't Star tell you? Several of our communities were attacked by these fiends."

"She told us."

"Did she inform you that it's believed two of the attacks took place on nights when the moon was full?"

"No, she neglected to tell us that news," Blade said. "So did Iron Wolf."

"Iron Wolf? I know him. Did he visit your Home?"

Blade nodded grimly. "He came with us to Yellowstone."

"Then where is—?" Eagle Feather began, and frowned. "What happened?"

"He was gored by a buffalo."

"I'm sorry to hear that. He was highly respected," Eagle Feather remarked. "Perhaps, since the moon wasn't a factor in other attacks, Star and Iron Wolf didn't regard the moon as part of a pattern."

"And you do?"

The Flathead shrugged. "When a man is desperate, he'll grasp at any straw."

Blade said nothing. He finished climbing to the top, where Hickok stood waiting, and surveyed their surroundings. A mule deer carcass had been deposited in the center of the level summit, and a stack of limbs to be used as firewood lay nearby. Visibility extended for miles in every direction. He could see the meandering course of the Lamar River to the northwest and the Absaroka Range to the east. "This is perfect," he commented.

"That's what I thought," Eagle Feather said.

Blade gazed to the southeast. He could distinguish vague figures moving about on the plain across the river. Harmon and his band were still working on the slain buffalo. He reasoned that the band would probably camp there for the night.

"Are they the scavengers?" Eagle Feather queried.

"Yep." Blade placed his vest and the T-shirt on the ground.

"I watched them go after the buffalo, and then the dust became so thick I couldn't tell what was happening."

"Do they know you're in this vicinity?"

"No. I've avoided them like the plague. I figured they'd kill me if they knew I was here."

"Wise decision."

"We should've blown those turkeys away when we had the chance," Hickok spoke up.

"We still may get the chance," Geronimo observed, and looked at the buck. "Why don't you and I start on that deer?"

"Fine by me," the gunman said.

"Be my guest," Eagle Feather stated, and drew his hunting knife. "Here. Use this."

"Thanks," Geronimo responded, and took hold of the hilt. "We'll have supper in no time."

"What can I do?" Achilles asked eagerly.

"Get a fire going," Blade ordered.

"Won't those scavengers see the smoke?"

"If they come to investigate, we'll sic Hickok on them," Blade proposed.

"I hope they do," the gunman said. "I'm rarin' for some real action."

Geronimo looked at him. "Real action? What do you call the buffalo stampede and the grizzly?"

"Appetizers."

Eagle Feather stared intently at Hickok. "Forgive me if I'm out of line, but I couldn't help but notice that you seem to like to kill."

"Killin' is part of the job. Nothin' more, nothin' less."

"Do you view being a Warrior as a mere job?"

"What would you call it?" Hickok rejoined, and continued before the Flathead could speak. "Being a Warrior is no different or better than being a Tiller or a Weaver. Oh, we have a little more responsibility because we're safeguarding lives, not crops, but when you get down to the nitty-gritty, Warriors kill for a livin'. We spend hours and hours practicing with our weapons just so we can wipe out the bad guys when the time comes to slap leather. We're trained killers." He glanced at Achilles. "If you start glorifying this job, you'll lose your perspective."

"My initial impression of you was clearly wrong," Eagle Feather said respectfully. "You might well be a killer, but you also possess much wisdom. The Family must regard you very highly, as my own people revere anyone who is a deep thinker and a seeker of truth."

For a few seconds Hickok appeared to be trying to catch flies in his mouth. He straightened, blinked, and glanced imperiously at Geronimo. "Deep thinker, huh?"

Geronimo closed his eyes and bowed his head. "I'm doomed. I'll never hear the end of this."

"Did I say something wrong?" Eagle Feather asked.

Hickok chuckled. "Nope. As a matter of fact, I can see now why the Flatheads control Montana and the Blackfeet don't."

"But the Blackfeet left Montana," Eagle Feather noted.

"That's just their excuse," Hickok stated. He walked

toward the buck, casting a haughty gaze at Geronimo. "Coming, mental midget?"

Geronimo looked at the Flathead. "Thanks heaps. What did I ever do to you?"

"I don't understand."

"I might as well find the nearest cliff and jump off," Geronimo muttered, turning away. "He'll be unbearable for at least six months."

"Let's go, peasant," Hickok called out.

"Make that a year," Geronimo amended, moving away as if stepping to the guillotine.

Eagle Feather faced the giant. "What did I do?"

"Nothing much, except give Hickok enough ammunition to last him a long time," Blade responded.

Perplexed, Eagle Feather glanced at the man in the red cloak. "Do you understand what is going on?"

Achilles sighed. "Unfortunately, yes."

"Would you explain it to me?"

"Were you ever five years old?"

"Of course. Everyone was."

Achilles pointed at Hickok and Geronimo. "So are they."

"Oh."

Smiling, Achilles pivoted and went to stretch, staring toward the river. He checked his movement and grasped the Bullpup in both hands. "Company is coming!" he announced.

Rapidly nearing the hill at a gallop was a white horse bearing a rider, a raven-tressed woman who unexpectedly shouted at the top of her lungs, "Help me! Or they'll kill me!"

Accenting her plea, four men appeared several hundred yards away, riding hard to overtake her.

CHAPTER TEN

"Fan out!" Blade ordered, moving to the rim. "Cover her."

Hickok and Geronimo moved to the giant's right, Achilles and Eagle Feather to his left.

"Do you want me to take out those cow chips after her?" the gunfighter asked.

"Not until I give the word," Blade responded, watching the woman. He seemed to recall seeing her earlier with Harmon's band. She rode expertly, her body hugging the horse as it raced for the hill, her waist-length hair streaming in the wind.

The four men were gaining, but only slightly.

In moments the white horse reached the slope and the woman goaded her mount upward. She was wearing a ragged brown shirt, torn jeans, and moccasins. "Don't shoot!" she cried nervously, eyeing their weapons.

"Stop, bitch!" bellowed one of the quartet pursuing her.

The woman reined up less than three yards from the bare-chested giant and leaped to the ground. "You've got to help me!" she stated, her green eyes pleading with him. "They'll kill me if they take me back.''

"Who are you?" Blade demanded.

"Priscilla. Priscilla Wendling."

"Aren't you one of Harmon's band?"

"No. Yes. Well, I was, but only because they forced me to stay with them," Priscilla said, glancing fearfully at the four men. "Please don't let them take me!"

Blade hesitated, studying her closely, speculating on whether her plea was genuine or a ruse. Finally he nodded. "Get behind us."

"Thank God!" Priscilla blurted out, and hurried onto the summit.

"Howdy, ma'am," Hickok said.

The four riders slowed, advancing cautiously, each man carrying a firearm, a rifle, or a revolver. In the lead rode a thin man attired in a green shirt and black pants. His head had been shaved bald and a golden earring hung from his left ear.

"I'll explain everything if you'll just save me from them," Priscilla promised, moving behind the giant.

"They're not taking you anywhere," Blade assured her, his flinty gaze on the quartet. He waited until they were starting up the slope before taking a pace forward. "That's far enough!" he warned.

The four men stopped, and the man sporting the earring brandished a rifle. "This doesn't concern you, chump."

"It does now."

"Are you the one called Blade?"

"I am."

"Listen, man. Harmon told us that he doesn't want any trouble with you. But that chick is ours and she's going back with us."

"She's yours?"

"Yeah. She's Harmon's squeeze. She was supposed to ride to the river and fill her canteen with water, but she kept going. Tricky bitch. Now we've got to take her to Harmon."

'She's not going with you," Blade stated.

Earring scowled and glanced at his companions, then

glared up at the giant. "You don't know what you're doing, man."

"I know perfectly well what I'm doing."

"Harmon ain't going to like this."

Blade smiled. "I don't *care* whether Harmon likes it or not. The woman is staying with us. If Harmon wants to see her, he can come here."

Earring had both his hands on his rifle. "What if we just take her sorry ass?"

"You can try."

For a few seconds Earring sat motionless on his horse, apparently weighing the odds. He shrugged and started to turn his mount. "She's Harmon's squeeze. He can come get her."

"Smart move," Blade said.

The three other riders went to leave.

Blade lowered the Commando barrel, thinking he had intimidated the scavengers, expecting them to ride off to notify their leader. He watched them, though, vigilant just in case, and it was well he did because Earring suddenly twisted in the saddle and swept the rifle up.

Someone else was faster.

Hickok's Henry cracked, the shot striking Earring in the middle of the forehead and knocking the scavenger to the ground. The gunman shifted to cover the other three. "Do you want one of these pills?" he taunted them.

None of them moved.

"Go tell Harmon how things are now," Blade directed. "Tell him we'll be waiting." He pointed at the body. "And take that piece of garbage with you."

The trio swiftly dismounted and draped Earring over his saddle, then climbed on their own animals and rode to the southeast, dust swirls rising behind them.

"Those clowns will be back," Hickok predicted.

Blade turned and stared at Prescilla Wendling. "Let's hear your story."

"What do you want to know?" she responded nervously.

"Everything. Let's start with where you're from."

"Vernal, Utah."

The Warrior's forehead creased, his curiosity aroused. "We've heard that the Mormons took over Utah after the war," he mentioned.

"They did. Lock, stock, and barrel. No one enters or leaves the state without the permission of bishops or the First President. But the Mormon Army patrols can't be everywhere, and the borders are constantly raided by scavengers. Harmon and his band hit Vernal eight years ago and kidnapped me. I've been with them ever since."

"How old are you?"

"Twenty-two."

"So you've been with them since you were about fourteen?"

"Yes," Priscilla answered sadly.

"And this is the first chance you've had to escape?" Blade asked skeptically.

Priscilla astutely perceived the implication. "Don't think I haven't wanted to get away! Do you really believe I like to have Harmon pawing me practically every night?" She paused, her countenance mirroring her inner torment. "That bastard rarely lets me out of his sight, and even then he always has someone watching me. The band hides out in remote areas like Yellowstone when they're not conducting raids. Anyone unfortunate enough to run into Harmon usually winds up dead."

"I reckon we have the proof we need," Hickok said, interrupting harshly.

"Proof?" Priscilla responded.

"Never mind," Blade said. "Go on."

Her shoulders slumped. "I suppose I could have snuck away during the night, but we're hundreds of miles from Vernal, and with all the wild animals, mutations, and degenerates roaming the countryside, I doubt I could make it on my own."

Blade digested the information inscrutably. Her tale was plausible. If Harmon had enshrined her as his favorite, the bastard undoubtedly would have kept a hawkish eye on her.

And he knew from bitter experience the horrific dangers populating the wilderness areas and rampant in the Outlands. He'd barely survived is own sojourns into the barbaric realms where bestial might made right, so he couldn't fault her judgment in not wanting to travel to Utah alone.

"I thought for sure that all of you were goners when Harmon spotted you," Priscilla related. "I was shocked when he let you live. No one has ever made him back down before."

"Do you have relatives living in Vernal?" Blade inquired.

"I did," Priscilla replied, and pursued her lips. "My mom and dad were killed by Harmon's bunch. I had an uncle and an aunt living in Vernal, but I don't know if they're still there." She gazed wistfully to the south. "If I was courageous, I would have committed suicide long ago."

"Don't talk like that. It's a lot easier to give up when the going gets rough than it is to face your difficulties head-on and persevere," Blade said. "You did what you had to do under the circumstances."

"Sometimes I wonder."

"As you pointed out, the odds of your successfully returning to Utah by yourself were almost nil. You might have attempted to find another inhabited town, but you would have been in the same fix. Other than killing Harmon in his sleep, your options were limited."

"I thought about killing the son of a bitch every night. I'd lie there, looking at him, and imagine myself slitting his throat. But I knew those cruds with him would torture me to death if I touched a hair on his head. If I'd tried to slip away, they would have trailed me to the ends of the earth."

Achilles unexpectedly walked over to her and performed a stately bow. "We haven't been formally introduced, Ms. Wendling. I'm Achilles, and I'd be honered if you would accept my services in your behalf."

"Your services?"

"Yes. Allow me to serve as your protector until such time as you are safely delivered to Vernal."

Priscilla gazed intently at the muscular man in the red

cloak. "Are you serious?"

"Never more so," Achilles assured her. "The indignities you've been forced to bear demand that justice be administered, and I'm just the man to see that justice is done."

"Modest, isn't he?" Geronimo quipped.

"Well, thank you, Achilles," Priscilla said. "I'm flattered. I've forgotten what it's like to be in the company of a true gentleman."

Hickok snickered. "Oh, brother."

"Pay no attention to these Neanderthals," Achilles advised her. "Perfect manners are not one of their strong suits."

"You remind me a lot of my Uncle Hiram," Priscilla said. "He was a strong, cultured man like yourself. He possessed the largest collection of books in the town, and he was always bringing me volumes to read when I was young." She paused. "That's another reason Harmon kept me around. I can read."

"He can't?" Blade queried.

Priscilla shook her head. "He's as illiterate as a rock."

"What a marvelous sense of humor," Achilles said, smiling broadly.

"Kiss her feet, why don't you?" Hickok muttered.

"The altitude must have gotten to him," Geronimo speculated.

"Perhaps, after this affair has been concluded, you would permit us to escort you to Utah," Achilles said. "Or you can accompany us to the Home."

"Where's the Home?"

"Achilles," Blade stated sternly.

Startled, the aspiring Warrior looked at the giant. "What did I do?"

"Whether we escort her to Utah will be *my* decision," Blade declared. "And information concerning the Home is privileged."

"It is?" Achilles responded in surprise.

"That's okay," Priscilla said. "I understand. Blade doesn't trust me yet."

"I don't know you," Blade said. "Until I do, the exact location of the Home must be our secret."

"Surely you don't believe she'd betray us," Achilles said.

"When you've been a Warrior as long as I have, you learn not to trust anyone until they've proven themselves to your satisfaction," Blade observed. "I know her story sounds very convincing, but there's a remote possibility that she's a plant, that Harmon sent her up here to learn what she could about us."

"I believe her," Achilles declared firmly.

"And I'd like to believe her," Blade replied.

Eagle Feather abruptly coughed loudly. "There's one way you can determine if she's telling the truth," he said.

Blade glanced at the Flathead. "How's that?"

Eagle Feather nodded to the southeast. "Ask Harmon. Here he comes."

Pivoting, Blade spied a group of riders racing toward the Lamar River. "Everyone check your weapons," he ordered, and inspected the Commando, insuring the cocking handle was all the way back.

"Can we open up as soon as they're in range?" Hickok asked hopefully.

"No. We'll hear what he has to say first."

The gunman shook his head and smacked his lips a few times. "You're gettin' soft in your old age, pard."

"We're the same age."

"Don't remind me. I'm liable to start sproutin' gray hairs any day now."

Achilles came forward and stood between the giant and the Flathead. He gazed at the head Warrior. "I apologize if I overstepped my bounds."

"You're forgiven. Officially you're not a Warrior yet, so I can't expect you to know all the rules of conduct."

"I have so much to learn."

"Comes with the territory," Blade said. "A Warrior's outlook on life must be different from the attitude most of the Family possesses. We can't afford to be as trusting, as spiritually loving. It's all well and good to believe in the

Golden Rule, to try and be kind to everyone as the Elders
teach us to do. But out here most people are looking out for
number one, and if you're not careful, someone you take
into your confidence could stab you in the back. Always be
on your guard, both physically and psychologically.''

"I'll try my best."

Blade saw the riders splash across the river and head
toward the hill. He knew the trio returning with Earring's
corpse had not had the time to reach the plain where the
buffalo were being butchered, and he surmised that Harmon
probably had become impatient and met them en route. He
held the Commando loosely at his side and waited for the
scavengers to arrive.

This time things would be different.

This time Harmon wouldn't leave alive.

CHAPTER ELEVEN

The 13 riders, with Harmon in the lead, slowed to a walk at the base of the hill, then came on slowly. Twelve, counting the big man, were men. The sole woman, a brunette in a seedy green blouse and beige slacks, hung back, glancing nervously at the summit.

Blade wanted all of them within a guaranteed kill radius. He let them ride to within 15 yards of the crest, then held his left hand aloft. "Stop right there!" he barked.

The scavengers reined up.

"What do you want?" Blade asked with feigned innocence.

"You know damn well what we want!" Harmon snapped. "Turn over my woman!"

"She's not your woman. Never has been."

Incipient rage contorted the scavenger's cruel visage. "Priscilla! Get your ass down here now!"

"Get stuffed!" she replied arrogantly.

Harmon leaned forward and glanced at the giant. "Do you think I'm playing a game? If you don't turn her over, there will be hell to pay."

"You're right about payment being due," Blade said.

"What?"

"Earlier, when I accused you of being a scavenger, you wanted to know where my proof was. Remember?"

Harmon straightened and placed his right hand on the Marlin resting on his thighs. "Yeah, I remember. So what?"

Grinning triumphantly, Blade pointed at Priscilla Wendling. "There's all the proof I need."

The scavenger snorted. "Big frigging deal. What are you going to do about it?"

"By the authority vested in me by the Freedom Federation, I could take all of you into custody."

Harmon smirked. "You could try."

"We're not going to bother," Blade informed him.

"You're not?" Harmon stated sarcastically. "Why? Afraid of the odds?"

"No," Blade said slowly, giving the scavenger ample opportunity to comprehend his meaning before he even uttered the words, his level gaze boring into the man's eyes, a smirk curling his mouth. "We're going to kill you."

For a moment no one moved. The scavengers all tensed, waiting for their leader to react, and react he did.

"You bastard!" Harmon roared, and tried to bring his rifle into play.

Blade was ready. He simply elevated the Commando barrel and squeezed the trigger, feeling a supreme degree of grim satisfaction as the heavy slugs ripped into Harmon's torso, stitching the big man from the navel to the neck. The impact catapulted Harmon from his saddle and he crashed onto the ground.

Hickok, Geronimo, Achilles, and Eagle Feather cut loose as the rest of the scavengers snapped off shots.

A few of the horses whinnied as they were accidentally hit. Other mounts were bucking or trying to flee, terrified by the gunfire, making it impossible for their riders to get a bead on the men on the rim.

Blade dove, firing as he did, and saw another scavenger tumble to the turf. He rolled to the right, striving to present as difficult a target as he could, and glimpsed Geronimo likewise hitting the dirt. Bullets smacked into the earth within inches of his head. He halted on his stomach and aimed at a thin man on a roan, who looked in his direction just as he sent a half-dozen rounds into the scavenger's chest.

Five of the band suddenly took the offensive. They goaded their animals upward, shooting as they charged, several of them uttering frenzied whoops and inarticulate yells.

Blade sighted on the scavenger in the lead and felt the Commando's recoil when the machine gun blasted.

Screeching, the rider fell to the slope and was kicked in the head by one of the other horses.

The brunette had wheeled her mount and fled toward the river.

Blade saw one of the scavengers coming toward him from the left, and he twisted to shoot before the rider did. He heard the booming of Achilles' Bullpup, and the scavenger's face erupted in a gory spray of flesh and blood.

The man toppled from his mount.

Human bodies and three dead or dying horses now littered the slope. Only four of the band were still alive, and two of them were endeavoring to turn their panicked animals and escape.

Hickok suddenly raced toward the four scavengers, his rifle discarded, a Colt Python in each hand. The revolvers spoke twice. In an uncanny, consummately lethal display of ambidextrous precision, he shot all four. As always, he went for the head. As always, four men fell with slugs in their brains.

A heavy silence descended on the hill.

"What a bunch of wimps," Hickok remarked, and twirled the Pythons into their holsters.

"We were lucky," Geronimo said, rising slowly, his eyes roving over the sprawled forms, checking for signs of life.

"Luck had nothin' to do with it," Hickok observed. "It was skill. They couldn't shoot straight worth beans."

"I wouldn't say that," Achilles declared.

Everyone swung toward the man in the red cloak, who was kneeling alongside Priscilla Wendling.

"How bad is she?" Blade asked, hurrying over to them.

The Mormon woman was flat on her back, her face distorted in pain, a growing red stain on her right shoulder. "They nailed me good," she said hoarsely.

"Check her," Blade told Achilles, then pivoted. "Hickok, Geronimo, make sure the scavengers are all dead."

"And if we find one alive?" the gunman asked.

"You know what to do."

Hickok grinned. "My pleasure, pard."

"I'll put the horses out of their misery," Geronimo said.

"Go ahead," Blade said, then abruptly realized one of their own was unaccounted for and turned to the north.

Eagle Feather stood eight yards away, his Winchester at his side, his posture slightly stooped. He stared at the grass with a peculiar expression.

"Are you all right?" Blade inquired, moving toward the Flathead.

"I don't know," Eagle Feather answered, and shifted so the giant could see the bullet hole in his left thigh. "They nailed me too."

"Sit down," Blade instructed him. "We'll dress the wound."

Grimacing and grunting, the Flathead lowered himself to the turf with the Warrior's assistance. "Just patch me up the best you can. I can't afford to let this slow me down. I must find Morning Dew, Little Mountain, and Black Elk."

"We'll hunt for them in the morning," Blade said. "For now, take off your pants."

"I can't."

"Beg pardon?"

Eagle Feather nodded at Priscilla Wendling. "I can't take my pants off."

"Why not?"

"She might see me."

"So?"

"I have nothing to cover my privates."

"The shy type, huh?" Blade joked to put Eagle Feather at ease, and straightened. He walked to the spot where he had left his vest and the damp T-shirt and picked up both. Which one should he lend to Eagle Feather? He opted for the T-shirt. There was no way he'd ever wear the vest again if another man used it to cover his genitals. "Here we go," he stated, returning. "Use this. It's a little wet." He tossed the T-shirt to the Flathead.

"Thank you."

Three shots sounded from the slope.

Blade stepped to the edge and saw Geronimo standing over a black stallion. He could tell by the stocky Warrior's countenance that Geronimo did not enjoy disposing of the animals.

Hickok was prodding one of the fallen scavengers with his left toe. "Hey, this cow chip is still kickin'," he announced. His right Colt materialized in his hand and he thumbed the hammer. The revolver cracked, and the scavenger's head seemed to bounce up and down. "Not any more," the gunfighter said.

Leaning the Commando against his right leg, Blade donned the torn vest and gazed out over the valley. Far off, on the other side of the Lamar River, riding to the southeast, was the brunette. He wondered what she would do now that she was by herself.

"Blade!" Achilles called.

The giant turned and walked to Princilla's side. "What's the verdict?"

"See for yourself," Achilles replied, the Amazon in his right hand.

Blade squatted, noting the woman's brown shirt had been cut open at the shoulder, revealing a neat, crimson-rimmed bullet hole an inch below the collarbone. "Is the slug still in there?"

"I found an exit hole," Achilles reported. "None of her major arteries or veins have been severed."

"Then we'll get a fire going and cauterize the wound," Blade proposed. "We'll do her and Eagle Feather both."

"Cauterize," Priscilla repeated timidly. "Will it hurt? I have a very low threshold for pain."

"Would you rather develop an infection and die from gangrene?"

"No."

"Then we'll cauterize the bullet hole. And yes, it'll hurt like crazy."

Priscilla looked into his eyes. "You don't pull any punches, do you?"

"Not where lives are concerned."

"I should thank you for saving me from Harmon."

"No problem. Exterminating scavengers is our specialty," Blade said, and grinned. "Were any members of the band missing, out on a raid or whatever?"

"No," Priscilla replied. "You got all of them."

"No, we didn't," Blade corrected her. "Another woman got away. Who was she?"

"That would be Milly Odum. She was captured by those scum when she was only ten, and she's been with them ever since."

"Did she take part in the killing?"

"Milly? No way. Harmon made her the band's slave. She had to do anything any of the men told her, even sleep with a different bastard every night."

"The poor woman," Achilles interjected.

"Maybe we should round up one of the horses and send someone after her," Blade suggested.

"Milly would just run away from you," Priscilla said. "She doesn't trust a soul, or she didn't until she met me. The trauma turned her into a frightened rabbit. She's afraid of her own shadow."

"We can't leave her out there alone."

"Patch me up, and tomorrow I'll ride over to the camp Harmon set up and talk to her. She'll come back with me."

"We'll go with you," Blade stated. "And while we're there, we'll look for the body of the guy with the Earring. They didn't have time to bury it, so it must be somewhere between this hill and the scavenger camp. It'll draw predators like garbage draw flies."

"You mean Silas. He was the one your friend with the

fancy revolvers shot.''

"Hickok is my friend's name," Blade disclosed. He stood and started toward Eagle Feather. "Stay with her, Achilles."

"Gladly."

The giant stared at the Flathead's bare leg as he approached. Eagle Feather had removed the buckskin leggings and strategically positioned the T-shirt over his loins. "Let me have a look," Blade said.

"Be my guest."

Kneeling down, Blade carefully examined the hole. From the size, about the width of this thumb, he decided a large-caliber rifle had done the job. Blood still flowed copiously, which wasn't a good sign. "Can you lift your leg a bit?"

"Certainly," Eagle Feather responded. He gritted his teeth and painfully elevated his left thigh.

Blade felt relief at finding the point where the bullet had emerged, just underneath the left buttock. They wouldn't need to operate to remove the slug. But the continued blood loss worried him. Eagle Feather could very well bleed to death if the flow wasn't stopped. "Don't move," he cautioned.

"I'm not going anywhere."

Smiling, Blade hurried to the rim and observed Geronimo and Hickok attempting to round up the stray mounts. He jogged down the slope toward them. "Forget the horses. Come here."

The gunfighter and the Blackfoot took one look and came to meet the giant halfway.

"What's up, pard?" Hickok inquired.

"Eagle Feather will die if we don't stop the bleeding," Blade informed them. "And Priscilla needs her wound cauterized. We have to get a fire going right away. Geronimo, you take care of that. Hickok, start to work on that buck. A good meal will have everyone feeling terrific."

Hickok nodded at three horses 40 feet away. "They'll likely wander off if we don't catch them now."

"It can't be helped. Eagle Feather and Priscilla are more important."

"We're on our way," Geronimo said, and sprinted off. The gunman hesitated.

"Is something wrong?" Blade asked.

"Yeah."

"What?"

"I don't rightly know," Hickok declared, and frowned. He gazed at the plain below. "I can't put my finger on it, but I feel like that time we were in the Twin Cities and all those blamed Wacks were watchin' us, only we didn't know it at first."

Blade had learned to trust the gunfighter's instincts. He scanned their surroundings but saw nothing out of the ordinary. "If there is something out there, I doubt we'll have to worry until after the sun goes down."

Hickok glanced at the sun, which was descending toward the western horizon, and nodded. "I reckon so." He headed for the summit. "I'd best tell Geronimo to make that a *big* fire."

CHAPTER TWELVE

An hour after sunset the air became cool thanks to a stiff breeze from the west, a breeze that fanned the flickering red and orange flames and sent fiery sparks wafting into the atmosphere.

Blade sat on the south side of the fire, his arms looped around is legs, his chin resting on his knees, and poundered their predicament. The fire and the roast venison had done wonders for Priscilla and Eagle Feather and aided their recovery after the grueling cauterization. Blade had done the honors himself, using a red-hot firebrand on both of them, inserting the thin, glowing stick into their bullet holes as far as it would go, first from the front and then from the rear. Priscilla had tried her best, but the agony had caused her to cry out and swoon. Eagle Feather, to his credit, had refused to scream the first time, although he had broken into a sweat and trembled as if suffering from a grave illness. But when the first attempt had failed to staunch the loss of blood, Blade had reheated the firebrand and tried once more, inserting the stick even farther, and the Flathead had succumbed to the torment and passed out. The second cauterization had been successful.

The Warrior stared at the two of them, lying to the north of the blazing wood Geronimo had gathered earlier, and nodded. They should both live. He'd allowed them to rest for half an hour after the operation, until the venison had been cooked, then aroused them to partake of the succulent meat. Now they were both conversing with Achilles, who seemed to have attached himself to the Mormon woman. From the way Priscilla kept touching his arm and leaning close to him, she reciprocated fully. Blade grinned at the sight. He'd have to take Achilles aside after they returned to the Home and talk to the "true gentleman" about conducting a romance while on duty.

Novices!

Blade leaned back and looked at Hickok, who sat on his right, then rotated his head until he spied Geronimo, who was on guard duty and walking the perimeter.

The full moon had risen 40 minutes ago.

"Tomorrow we'll see if we can catch any of the horses and begin sweeping the area for sign of the Bear People," Blade said conversationally.

"The who?" Priscilla asked.

"Mutations. They abducted Eagle Feather's wife and two sons. The reason we're in Yellowstone is to find them and eliminate them," Blade explained.

"What do they look like?"

"No one knows for sure."

"I caught a glimpse of them," the Flathead disclosed. "I only know they are big and hairy and very, very clever."

"I wonder if they were involved in the disappearance of two of Harmon's men," Priscilla remarked.

Blade peered at her through the flames. "Two of his men vanished?"

"Yep. About a week ago. We never found a trace of them, but we did discover one of their horses. It had been partially eaten."

"Were any strange tracks found at the scene?" Blade asked.

"Not that I know of."

Could there be a connection? Blade wondered. The Bear People might have been responsible for the disappearance of the pair of scavengers, but a wild beast could just as well have done the job. He speculated on whether he had miscalculated. Maybe the creatures had already passed through the Lamar Valley and were now somewhere in central or southern Wyoming. If he'd—

"Blade! Hickok!" Geronimo suddenly shouted.

The giant leaped to his feet, grabbing the Commando as he stood. "Stay put," he directed the others, then nodded at the gunman and together they ran to their friend.

Geronimo was standing on the southeast side of the summit, the FNC cradled loosely, staring at something in the distance.

"What is it, pard?" Hickok asked.

"Did you hear something?" Blade added.

"I see something," Geronimo informed them. "A fire, to be precise." He lifted his right hand and pointed.

Blade spied the campfire before Geronimo's arm was extended. A solitary beacon of light in a virtual sea of shadowy landscape, the roaring blaze appeared to be three times the size of their own. He estimated the fire to be situated in the general vicinity of the slain buffalo. "It must be the other woman, Milly Odum," he commented.

"What the blazes is she tryin' to do?" Hickok questioned. "Set the countryside on fire?"

"She's probably scared being all by herself," Geronimo guessed. "I wouldn't be surprised if she keeps that fire going all night."

"How about if I mosey on down there and try and persuade her to join us?" Hickok proposed. "She shouldn't be all by her lonesome in a wilderness like this."

"You'd have to cover over three miles," Blade noted.

"So? I'm not afraid of the dark," Hickok responded. "Besides, with the full moon and all, it's not that bad."

Blade debated for a moment. "No, we'll all go in the morning. Priscilla told me that Odum will take off if we try to get near her, and we don't want her roaming around at night.''

"Suit yourself," Hickok said with a shrug.

"One of us will relieve you in a few hours," Blade said to Geronimo. He turned and took a few strides, then froze when his ears registered the far off sound.

A scream.

A primal, wavering, almost eerie scream, the unmistakable cry of a terrified woman, faint yet compelling in its intensity.

"Dear Spirit!" Geronimo exclaimed.

"I knew it," Hickok declared. "One of us should get down there, pronto."

Blade stepped to the crest and stared at the campfire. He thought he saw indistinct forms pass in front of the flames, but he couldn't be certain. "I'll go."

"Why you?" Hickok asked.

"Because rightfully it's my job. I'm the representative of the entire Federation in my capacity as the head of the Force," Blade said, feeling a twinge of guilt. If that woman had been a Family member, he would have gone after her. "I should have tried to contact her earlier. You were right."

"I was?" Hickok replied, and grinned. "Boy, am I on a roll."

"By the time you get down there, she'll probably be dead," Geronimo mentioned.

"I have to find out for myself," Blade stated.

"Take one of us with you, pard," Hickok said.

"Yeah," Geronimo said. "What if it's the Bear People?"

Blade swung toward their fire. "Achilles! Front and center on the double!"

"You're takin' the greenhorn?" Hickok declared in surprise.

"Why not one of us?" Geronimo questioned.

"He needs the experience. You don't. It's that simple," Blade explained. He spotted the aspiring Warrior racing their way. "I'll expect the two of you to keep watch over Priscilla and Eagle Feather. If you see or hear anything out of the ordinary, get off a few shots and we'll come running.''

"Just take care of yourselves," Geronimo said.

Achilles joined them. "What is it?" he asked excitedly, glancing around. "Are we being attacked?"

"You're going with me," Blade directed, and nodded to the southeast.

"And leave Priscilla?"

Hickok snickered. "Maybe Blade will let you carry her piggyback," he quipped.

"Let's go," Blade said, and headed down the slope.

Achilles took a few steps, then looked back at the gunfighter. "Take care of her, will you?"

"Don't fret your noggin'," Hickok responded. "We'll watch out for her."

"Thanks," Achilles said, and beamed. "She finds me fascinating. Not that I blame her."

"True love, huh?"

"I've never been in love before," Achilles confided. "But I do know I find her irresistibly exhilarating."

"Enjoy it while it lasts. After the first kid, you'll be lucky if you're exhilarated once a month."

"I don't understand."

"Figures."

From a dozen yards down the hill came an irate bellow. "Achilles!"

"Uh-oh. Be seeing you," Achilles said, and sprinted into the night.

Hickok glanced at Geronimo. "That boy is downright pitiful."

"Yeah. I know what you mean. He reminds me of you when you were his age."

"I was never that stuck on myself."

"I was referring to his ignorance."

"He does have a heap to learn about women, that's for sure."

"Yeah. And the more he learns, the less he'll know,"

Geronimo observed.

The gunman ambled off. "Give me a holler if a moth tries to beat you up."

"Try not to set your buckskins on fire."

Hickok chuckled and strolled to the fire, the Henry in his left hand.

Both the Flathead and the Mormon woman were sitting up.

"What happened?" Priscilla inquired anxiously. "Where's Achilles?"

"Blade and him went snipe-huntin'," Hickok said, and eased to the ground, lying the rifle on his left.

"At this time of night?"

"Yep. There's a whole herd of the critters down near the river. They wanted to bag a few for breakfast."

Priscilla glanced toward the east rim. "It's too dangerous to wander around after dark in Yellowstone." She paused and regarded the gunman suspiciously. "Wait a minute. Snipe hunting? I've never heard of snipes. What are they?"

"The meanest animals in the world."

"Do you mean Achilles could be hurt?"

"Knowin' snipes the way I do, they could tear him to itty-bitty pieces if he's not careful," Hickok said with a straight face. "But I wouldn't worry if I was you. He can take care of himself. And Blade will baby-sit him."

"Achilles doesn't need baby-sitting," Priscilla responded defensively. "He's a mature adult."

"Know him that well already, do you?"

"Let's just say I happen to like him."

"Do tell! I never would've guessed."

Priscilla reached up and rubbed her sore shoulder. "You're making fun of me, aren't you?"

"Who, me?"

"I think you're pulling my leg," Priscilla said. She looked at Eagle Feather. "Is Achilles in any danger?"

"From the snipes?"

"Of course. What else would I be talking about?"

"Are you sincerely concerned?"

"What kind of question is that?" Priscilla snapped.

Eagle Feather nodded. "Yes, you obviously care for him. And you shouldn't have to needlessly worry. No, Achilles is not in any danger."

"Thank you," Priscilla said, and stared at the Warrior. "You have a sick sense of humor."

"So everybody keeps tellin' me."

"Then why don't you change?"

"My missus likes me the way I am."

"*You're* married?"

"Yep. To the cutest filly this side of the Milky Way," Hickok stated proudly.

"Give her my condolences."

"Anyone ever tell you that you've got a nasty streak a yard wide?"

Priscilla smiled. "I wish it was true."

"Why?"

"I would have blown that bastard Harmon away years ago."

"Don't blame yourself. Most folks are naturally nice. There are some who are outright nasty just to be spiteful. And there are those who learn to be nasty when the chips are down, but even most of them don't cotton to the nastiness," Hickok said. "Get my drift?"

"I think so," Priscilla replied. "Which category do you belong to?"

"None of them."

"None?"

"I'm in the fourth category."

"Which is?"

"I've learned how to be nasty when the going gets rough, when lowlifes are tryin' to hurt decent folks or a crazed mutation is tryin' to rip someone's face off," Hickok stated, then grinned. "The difference is I *like* being nasty when nastiness is called for."

"You like exterminating lowlifes, as you call them?"

"Someone has to do the job."

"What about Achilles?" Priscilla asked.

"What about him?"

"Does he like being nasty?"

"I wouldn't know. I haven't seen him against the wall yet."

"Against the wall?"

Hickok nodded and gazed into the fire. "That's when everything is going wrong, and you find yourself outnumbered with your back to the wall. It's either you or the other guy. Or things. And it's then, when the lives of others are ridin' on your shoulders and you know a lot of good people will die if you don't get your act together, that you have to become nasty, become as mean as you can be, just to stay alive. As far as I know, Achilles hasn't been in that kind of situation yet. He's never had to be nasty."

"Well, I hope he never finds his back to the wall."

"And I hope he does."

"Why on earth would you wish such a thing on any man?"

"Because it's the true test of whether he's cut out to be a Warrior. Until he learns whether he's got the guts to do whatever it takes to beat the bad guys, he'll never know if he has what it takes to be a Warrior," Hickok said. He looked at her. "Our Elders don't pick just anyone to be a Warrior. There's a tough selection process every candidate goes through, and there's a reason. The Elders want to weed out the dreamers from the true fighters. It's real easy to sit in a comfy chair dreamin' about slayin' dragons, but to go out and actually kill the dragon takes more guts than most folks realize."

"Truly you are a wise man," Eagle Feather interjected.

Hickok laughed. "Could I have that in writing?"

"Why?" the Flathead asked.

"Otherwise my misses will never believe it."

"You must love your wife very much."

"You bet. Don't you?" Hickok asked, and immediately regretted his lack of tact when Eagle Feather frowned and bowed his head.

"With all of my heart."

"Cheer up. We'll find her and the young'uns."

"I pray you are right."

They fell silent, each engrossed in his or her thoughts.

Hickok watched the flickering flames and thought about Sherry, Ringo, and Chastity. What were they doing right at that moment? Sherry was probably giving the kids their nightly baths, and he wished he could be there to play Navy with Ringo. A month ago he had traded a hunting knife for four carved wooden ships an Elder had whittled.

What was that?

Hickok stiffened and glanced to the south. He'd heard a soft thump, as if a horse had stomped its hoof. Or a body had struck the ground.

Where was Geronimo?

The gunfighter stood, his hands hovering near his Colts, and scanned the summit.

"Is something wrong?" Priscilla asked.

"Nope," Hickok fibbed. He didn't want to alarm her unnecessarily. "I'll be right back. I need to shoot the breeze with that mangy pard of mine."

"I saw him near the south rim a minute ago."

"Thanks," Hickok said, and walked away from the fire, probing the shadows for his friend's silhouette. The fire didn't illuminate the entire summit, but the full moon provided a pale glow along the outer edge. He should be able to spot Geronimo easily.

His fellow Warrior was nowhere in sight.

Hickok advanced to within a yard of the southern rim and halted. He felt confident that there wasn't an animal or mutation alive capable of sneaking up on Geronimo undetected, and he reasoned his friend had undoubtedly stepped down the slope to take a leak. "Pard?"

There was no answer.

The gunfighter took a pace, then abruptly stopped. Something didn't feel right. He couldn't put his finger on the cause. The night seemed serene. Stars filled the heavens, and off to the southeast Milly Odum's fire still blazed. "Geronimo?" he called out.

Again there was no reply.

Hickok decided to check the slope below. But first he'd better let Priscilla and Eagle Feather know he'd be gone for a few minutes. He pivoted and hastened toward the fire, and he had ten feet to cover when his roving gaze chanced to alight on the exact spot where the Mormon and the Flathead had been resting.

They were gone.

For a second Hickok couldn't believe his own senses. He slowed, glancing every which way, certain they had to be on the summit. They wouldn't have gone anywhere, and if they'd been attacked at least one of them would have cried out.

So where were they?

Hickok stood still, listening, thoroughly confounded. A whisper of a noise was borne to his ears by the breeze, the merest hint of a footfall to his rear, the scraping pressure of a calloused pad on a blade of grass, and he tensed.

What a chump!

How could he have been so dumb?

The gunfighter whirled, executing his lightning draw as he completed the revolution, both Colts streaking up and out, and there they were, five or six hulking, hunched-over forms closing on him from behind, their facial features indistinguishable in the gloom.

One of the things snarled and leaped.

Hickok snapped off a shot from each Python, and he saw the creature somersault backwards as if slammed in the head by an invisible sledgehammer.

Another thing rushed at him, and another.

Hickok squeezed off two quick shots, the slugs tearing into the foremost attacker, causing the thing to stumble and almost go down. Incredibly, the creature recovered its balance and bounded forward. Hickok thumbed back the hammer, about to send two more shots into his adversary, when the unexpected transpired.

Steely arms encircled him from behind, pinning his arms to his sides.

He'd neglected to cover his rear!

Hickok felt warm breath on his neck and inhaled a fetid odor. He strained to break free, but the arms restraining him were like the unbreakable coils of a huge boa constrictor. Lifting his legs, he began thrashing and kicking and butting his head into the thing holding him, hoping his violent motions would make the creature stumble or release him.

No such luck.

One of his attackers halted directly in front of him, not a foot and a half away.

Still struggling, Hickok glanced at the creature, and his initial impression was of hair. Lots and lots of hair. And teeth. Long, tapered teeth that were exposed when the thing growled and hissed at him.

A hand reached for the gunfighter's throat.

Do something! Hickok thought. His arms were pinned, but he could move his forearms a few inches and he did so now, slanting the Python barrels upwards. The angle prevented him from going for a head shot, so he did the next best thing. He simply pointed the Colts at the creature's midsection and fired.

The thing clutched at its stomach and staggered a few feet, then sank to its knees, inadvertently putting its head in a direct line with the Warrior's revolvers.

Hickok got off two more shots. Before he could witness the result, the creature holding him vented a bestial roar and hurled him to the hard ground. He landed on his left shoulder, grunting at the pain, and flipped onto his back to cut loose once more.

He never got off a shot.

The brutish beings rushed out of the night and swarmed all over him, coming from every direction, their heavy forms pouncing on his unprotected body. Hands gripped his wrists and others tore the Colts from his grasp. Malletlike fists struck him repeatedly, as the creatures battered him mercilessly on his head and chest. He struggled vainly to batter them aside so he could stand. A claw ripped his left cheek open. A knee gouged him in the stomach. He gasped for air and swung his fists to no avail.

An instant later a ten-ton boulder seemed to crash into his jaw and his universe faded to black.

CHAPTER THIRTEEN

The cool night invigorated Blade as he raced toward the Lamar River. He inhaled deeply, enjoying the exercise, his long legs flying over the terrain. The Bowies jiggled in their sheaths, and the Commando, which he had slung over his left shoulder, swayed from side to side, rubbing against his back. He trained his eyes on Odum's campfire and listened for another scream.

Except for insect noises, all was quiet.

Blade glanced over his right shoulder at Achilles. Fifteen feet separated them, and the novice appeared hard-pressed to keep up. "Quit goofing off and get up here," he commanded.

"Who's goofing off?" Achilles retorted, and increased his speed marginally. "Can I help it if you cover twice as much ground with each step?"

Grinning, Blade slowed to allow the aspiring Warrior to reach his side. "You must be out of shape."

"I'm in excellent condition," Achilles responded defensively.

"How many miles do you jog every day?"

"Five miles every other day."

"After we return to the Home, start a new exercise regimen and include doing ten miles every day."

Achilles glanced at the giant. "Every day?"

"Until you can comfortably keep up with me, yes."

"How do Hickok and Geronimo do it?"

"They have a secret."

"What is it?" Achilles inquired eagerly.

"They usually ask me to take little steps."

For a moment Achilles couldn't decide if the top Warrior was serious, then he voiced a hearty laugh. "No one at the Home could ever hope to match you on a long run."

"Yama and Rikki-Tikki-Tavi consistently tie with me," Blade mentioned. "And on short sprints, Rikki is even faster."

"I had no idea. What's the secret of their success?"

"They've developed their bodies to where they can perform at their maximum level," Blade said. "Although they're quite different in stature, they're both solid muscle."

"So is Samson," Achilles noted.

"But Samson has never had to lift a weight or exercise strenuously in his life. His physique matured naturally."

"Is he as fast as you are?"

"No, but he's equally as strong."

"I doubt that."

"Size alone is no prerequisite for the possession of great strength," Blade said. "Look at Rikki."

"I still can't accept that any of the other Warriors are as strong as you."

"Trust me. I've seen Samson in action. When he calls on the Lord for strength, none of us can rival him."

"Do you really believe that Nazarite mumbo jumbo?"

"Samson does. And whether you prefer to think that his immense power is psychologically triggered or stems from the Spirit, the fact remains that when Samson prays to the Lord, his strength is increased a hundredfold."

Achilles gazed at the river ahead. The surface of the water reflected the pale moonlight and resembled a wide ribbon of glass. A thought occurred to him and he almost stopped in surprise. "Wait a minute!" he blurted.

"What's wrong?" Blade asked, running effortlessly.

"Why are we doing all this talking? Shouldn't we approach the fire stealthily? Whatever attacked that poor woman will hear us."

"Good."

"Did I miss something here?"

"I want them to hear us," Blade stated. "I want them to come after us."

"I definitely missed something."

Blade grinned. The fact that Achilles possessed a sense of humor indicated the novice wasn't quite as egotistical as he seemed. "Think, Achilles. Think. Why did we travel all the way to Yellowstone?"

"To exterminate the mutations responsible for the raids on the Flatheads."

"Exactly. And we can't exterminate them if we can't *find* them. In which case we do the next best thing. We let them find us. If they're out there somewhere, they'll hear us and try to take us down."

"In other words, you're deliberately setting us up as bait?"

"Bingo."

"My apologies. I should have realized. Normally my deductive reasoning is superb."

"Not to mention your modesty," Blade said. He came to a halt 20 yards from the river and scrutinized the opposite shore. The thicket where the grizzly had been concealed presented a foreboding aspect, visible as a dark wall of inky vegetation. "We'll cross here and work our way southward along the other bank."

"Do you want me to jump up and down every few feet to attract attention?"

Blade smiled. "That won't be necessary," he replied, and walked to the edge of the water. "Just keep your eyes peeled."

"You don't have to tell me twice," Achilles assured him. He picked up the trailing edge of his red cloak, draping the lower half over his left arm. "Ready when you are."

Unslinging the Commando, Blade held the weapon at chest height and proceeded into the frigid water. He advanced gingerly, feeling his way with his feet, hoping to avoid slipping on a rock. Ten feet from the bank he abruptly halted.

A rustling noise arose in the thicket, a loud crackling of branches and swishing of leaves.

Blade pointed the Commando at the obscure mass of dense brush.

"What if it's a grizzly?" Achilles whispered.

"Don't miss."

The rustling suddenly ceased.

"Stay frosty," Blade advised, and took two strides. The next sounds he heard brought a tingle to his spine, and he spun and stared to the west.

There had been two shots.

Two shots blending almost as one.

"Hickok!" Blade exclaimed, and surged toward the west bank, stepping past Achilles, and even as he moved there were two more shots. "Let's go!"

Achilles started to follow when he detected movement on the east shore in the vicinity of the thicket. He hesitated, and a half-dozen shadowy figures materialized near the river.

The six creatures plunged into the water.

A hasty glance confirmed that Blade was almost to the shore. The giant seemed to have forgotten all else in his desire to reach the hill. Achilles looked at the things splashing toward him. He cooly leveled the Bullpup, aimed at the creature in the lead, and fired.

The blast knocked the figure into the river.

Grinning, Achilles backpedaled. Whatever they were, the creatures could be killed. His elation lasted all of five seconds, however.

The thing he had shot rose out of the water and resumed its pursuit.

Achilles moved faster. He shot another of the creatures and saw it go down, only to stand erect moments later. What in the world *were* they? he wondered, and bumped into the bank. A heavy hand fell on his right shoulder. Startled, he looked up.

"This is no time to go swimming with the natives," Blade said, and helped the younger man clamber onto the bank.

"They're still coming!" Achilles declared, his eyes on the six charging things.

"Let them," Blade said, and gave the novice a shove westward. "Run as you've never run before," he ordered, and took off, gratified when Achilles came alongside him on the right.

Two more shots sounded from the hill.

"Hickok and Geronimo must be holding their own," Achilles remarked breathlessly.

Blade didn't bother to respond. He conserved his energy, staring at the circle of light crowning the prominence, dreading that he had committed a monumental blunder by dividing his forces.

A large, vague shape suddenly came into view on the left, angling to intercept them.

"Blade!" Achilles cried in warning.

"I see it," the giant replied, and aimed the Commando on the run. He squeezed the trigger, shooting by instinct, and his aim turned out to be unerring.

The thing clutched at its torso and toppled.

Blade faced front, his legs pounding, his heart doing the same. What if he was too late? What if the mutations had killed his friends and the others? What if his blunder wound up costing lives, the lives of the two best friends he had?

"On the right!" Achilles shouted.

Blade glanced to the north and spotted two more of their assailants loping toward them. "Waste them!" he barked, and fired the Commando at the same instant Achilles cut loose with the Bullpup.

One of the creatures fell, but the second bounded closer.

Aiming carefully, Blade fired at the thing's head.

The other figure dropped.

Blade raced onward, scanning the field for more creatures. He gazed over his right shoulder and saw the mutation he'd just shot stand and sprint after them. Talk about *tough*! He looked at the hill and poured on the speed.

Achilles did likewise. "Go on ahead of me!" he urged.

"Be serious," Blade replied.

"You can run faster than I can. They might need you," Achilles said. "Priscilla could be in trouble."

"We'll stick together."

"But Priscilla—"

"Just move it!" Blade snapped. He scanned the field to the right and the left, relieved to note none of the creatures were trying to overtake them. But there was still the one to their rear. He looked back again, and felt momentarily disconcerted at discovering the thing had vanished.

What was going on?

A minute elasped without incident and they reached the base of the hill safely.

"Cover my back!" Blade ordered, and sped toward the summit, fearing he would find the worst, afraid everyone would be dead. He swept over the rim and crouched, the Commando tucked against his right side, ready to combat all comers.

But there was no one to fight.

Not a soul was in sight. Hickok, Geronimo, Priscilla, and Eagle Feather were all gone. Only the fire still pulsed with a life of its own, its fingers of flame dancing heavenward.

"Where are they?"

Blade looked at the novice, who stood on the crest, and shook his head.

"They took Priscilla?"

"They took everybody," Blade corrected him. A glint of firelight off a gleaming object in the grass near the fire drew his attention. He hastened over and bent down to find both of Hickok's Pythons lying on the ground. The presence of the revolvers filled him with anxiety. Hickok never went anywhere without those guns. There was even a joke currently making the rounds, started by Geronimo, to the effect that the gunfighter even wore his prized Colts when he made whoopee.

Achilles walked to the fire, evidently stunned by the disappearances. "They took everybody?" he repeated absently.

"Check for weapons," Blade directed.

"What?"

"Weapons, man. Weapons. The creatures didn't take the weapons. We'll need every one we can find."

"Right away," Achilles said, grateful for the chance to do something, anything, so he wouldn't need to dwell on Priscilla's probable fate.

Blade picked up the Pythons and stuck them under his belt. Nearby he found the Henry and slung the rifle over his left shoulder.

"Here's the FNC and Geronimo's Arminius," Achilles announced, waving the firearms.

"You'll have to carry them," Blade stated. He started to make a circuit around the fire, moving in ever-widening circles as he searched for weapons and clues to the direction the attackers had taken.

Achilles walked in a zigzag pattern to the north. He spotted a long object partly concealed by the grass and stooped down to grab it. A brief inspection sufficed to reveal the object was a Winchester with a shattered stock. "Hey, look at this," he declared.

Blade stepped over and took the gun. He examined the stock for a few seconds, then hefted the rifle. "This is Eagle Feather's. Insteresting, isn't it, that they threw all the guns away."

"How so?"

"Guns are at a premium everywhere. If human raiders had been responsible for this ambush, they would have taken all the guns and left bodies. But these Bear People, these mutations, obviously couldn't care less about weapons. They prefer to rely on their mutant abilities, on their strength and speed."

"Maybe the things are too stupid to know how to operate a firearm," Achilles speculated.

"Maybe, but somehow I doubt it," Blade said. He tossed the Winchester aside.

"Shouldn't we take it with us?" Achilles asked. "The stock can always be repaired."

"I know, but we'll have our hands full as it is," Blade replied. "We'll cover the Winchester with deer hide and come back for it after we find out what's happened to the others," Blade proposed, and surveyed the summit. "Wait a minute. Where's the buck?"

"What?"

"The mule deer Eagle Feather shot. The buck was carved up for supper. There was a lot left over," Blade observed. "Where did the carcass go?"

Achilles looked around. "They took it."

Frowning, Blade moved closer to the fire. "We'll spend the rest of the night here. I'll take the first watch."

"We're not going after them?"

Blade glanced at the novice. "Which way would we go?"

Bafflement etched Achilles' features. He turned to the north, then the south. "I don't know," he admitted.

"There's nothing we can do until daylight," Blade said. "We can't track them at night. At first light we'll scour the hill and the plain for sign. If we're lucky, we'll find tracks."

"And if we don't discover any tracks?"

"Then we'll have no way of knowing the direction they took," Blade answered, his broad shoulders drooping, "and we may never see Hickok and Geronimo again."

CHAPTER FOURTEEN

Strange.

He couldn't remember a mountain falling on him, and yet that was exactly how he felt.

Every muscle in his body ached. He seemed to be one large bruise, from the hairs on his head to the tips of his toes. What could have happened? His mind was sluggish, his memory fuzzy. Had his missus gotten ticked off because he'd let the kids play World War Three in the living room again?

Somebody had sure stomped him, but good.

He became conscious of a peculiar swaying movement and felt cool air on his cheeks and brow.

Where was he, anyway?

A rank odor assailed his nostrils. He became aware of being bent in half at the waist. When he opened his eyes, he thought for a moment he must be dreaming.

Why was he lying on a hairy rug?

Better yet, why was the rug moving?

Suddenly insight dawned and he recalled the battle on the hill. The blamed critters must have captured him!

How embarrassing!

Well, at least he should look at the bright side. He was still alive. So to speak. He attempted to move his dangling arms and found his wrists had been securely bound.

Figured.

He realized he had been draped over someone's shoulder. Correction. Make that something's shoulder. The creatures were carting him somewhere. Why? What did they have in mind? He wondered about the others. Were they still alive too, or had the critters killed them?

What should he do next?

He could feel an arm encircling his waist. By kicking and lunging forward, he might be able to break loose. Might. Whatever was carrying him must be immensely strong, if the ease with which the thing conveyed his 180 pounds served as any indication.

Someone groaned.

He twisted his head, listening carefully. Far overhead, the starry firmament stretched into infinity. So it was still night, and he probably hadn't been unconscious very long.

The groan was repeated.

Relief made him smile. Would the creatures object if he spoke? There was only one way to find out. "Pard, is that you?"

"Hickok?"

"Yep. Are you okay?"

"Something is carrying me."

"You Injuns never fail to amaze me with your powers of observation."

"Suck eggs."

A new voice interrupted their conversation. "Hickok! Geronimo! It's me, Priscilla."

"Where's Eagle Feather?" Hickok inquired, but he never received an answer.

"Shut your mouth!" someone commanded in a gruff, raspy tone. "The next one of you scum who talks will have his tongue ripped out!"

Hickok almost told the speaker to go to hell. Instead, he fell silent and pondered his predicament. There was no sense in trying to escape until he knew what was going on, so he resigned himself to playing along for the time being. But sooner or later he would have a reckoning with the critters that clobbered him.

Provided they didn't kill him first.

CHAPTER FIFTEEN

A rosy tinge enveloped the eastern horizon and radiated upward and outward, heralding the arrival of a new day, the signal for the sparrows and starlings and other birds in Yellowstone to greet the dawn in their own inimitable manner, by chirping and singing in a boisterous avian chorus.

Blade sat on the east side of the fire, staring at the low flames and the burning embers, and inhaled deeply. Morning at last! He'd been unable to catch a wink of sleep all night. How could he doze off when the creatures might return? How could he take even a short nap when Hickok and Geronimo were in danger of losing their lives, if they hadn't already? Not to mention Priscilla and Eagle Feather. The thought of the Mormon woman prompted him to glance to his right.

Achilles hadn't slept either. He'd spent all night walking around the rim of the hill. Around and around and around. Now he was moving along the north edge, his visage downcast, dragging his heels.

"Are you ready?" Blade asked.

"Finally!" Achilles responded, halting and stretching. "Yes, I'm ready. I can't wait to catch the things that took

Priscilla.''

"And the others,'' Blade noted dryly.

"Of course. I want to rescue them too.''

"I'm happy to hear it,'' Blade said. He stood and surveyed the countryside. To the south, a quarter of a mile distant, were four large animals. Buffaloes, he assumed, until he took a closer look and distinguished the distinctive outlines and flowing tails of a godsend. "Horses!''

"Where?'' Achilles inquired, hurrying over.

Blade pointed. "Go get them while I check for tracks.''

"On my way,'' Achilles replied, running off.

The giant stood watching the novice jog down the slope, then turned and stepped to the north rim. He slowly proceeded westward around the outer circumference, intently examining the ground for prints. Unfortunately, grass covered almost every suare inch of earth, minimizing the possibility of discovering an impression. He deduced that the things had departed either to the north, west, or south because he and Achilles had been to the east and hadn't spied the creatures leaving with their burdens. Of course, the things could have slipped past unseen.

Blade paused. Another factor to consider was the direction of travel the mutations had been taking before the attack last night. The creatures had been bearing in a south-southeasterly direction, and they might still be on the same course.

Might.

Then again, they might not.

Perturbed, he reached a point due west of the smoldering fire and noticed a saucerlike depression of dirt at the base of the hill. What could have happened to the grass? he wondered, and ran toward the depression. He vaguely recalled reading that buffaloes often formed dusty wallows in which they rolled and rubbed repeatedly. This must be one.

The depression was ten feet in width, and the earth had been churned into clods by the constant tramping of heavy hoofs.

Blade halted next to the wallow, noting the scores of hoof-prints in the dirt and around the border. He knelt and scrutinized the earth for different prints. If the creatures had fled in this direction, they might not have noticed the wallow in the dark. Or they might not have viewed the leaving of tracks as anything to become worried about. In any event, if he could find just one clear print he'd know which way they went.

He found five.

They were all along the north side of the wallow, crossing from east to west, blending into the buffalo prints so well he didn't notice them at first. Five prominent toes were the giveaway, and he moved around the border and squatted to examine the footprints.

How grotesque.

Blade had done a fair amount of hunting and tracking in his lifetime, and never had he beheld the like. They appeared to be a cross between a human print and a bear track, which fit the description supplied by Star and Iron Wolf.

The Bear People.

The bastards.

He stood and walked back up the slope, debating his next move and trying to rationalize the intent of the creatures. Why were the things now heading westward after traveling southward for so many miles? Were they trying to throw off any pursuit? Did the things intend to double back later? What was his best option? Go west? Or go south?

Blade came to the crest and stopped. Tracking the mutations promised to be a difficult and arduous task. It would entail scouring every foot of exposed earth en route on the off chance one of the creatures had goofed and left a print. Such a procedure would be wearisome and time-consuming, and time was a commodity they were short on.

But what choice did they have?

He moved to the fire and stared idly at the last of the flames, chiding himself for his performance. He should never have divided his forces! If only that woman hadn't screamed . . .

The woman!

Milly Odum!

Blade gazed to the southeast. He'd forgotten all about her in the heat of events. What if she was lying down there, injured? Or what if she had escaped the creatures and was now hiding in the general area? Should he ride to the scavenger camp before heading out after his friends, Eagle Feather, and Priscilla?

What was he thinking?

The plain where the buffaloes had been slain must be three or four miles distant. Precious time would be consumed in the ride there and back. He had to be practical. The odds that Odum had escaped the mutations was virtually nil. The creatures had undoubtedly captured her, as well. So venturing to the camp would serve no useful purpose.

Still, what if he was wrong?

Blade shook his head, his lips tightening. He had to be firm. He had to weigh which course of action would achieve the greatest good. Giving chase to the mutations must be his paramount priority. If it later developed that he'd been in error, then he could indulge in self-recrimination. Personal failings were best reflected in the mirror of one's own soul in private.

The faint sound of drumming hoofs reached his ears.

He hastened to the south rim and saw Achilles galloping toward the hill astride a brown stallion, the red cloak streaming in the wind, leading another horse, a black gelding, by the reins. Eager to get underway, he jogged to meet the younger man halfway.

"The other two ran off," Achilles announced as he drew nearer. "I assumed you didn't want me to waste time trying to catch them."

"You were right," Blade stated.

"With the horses we should overtake the mutations quickly," Achilles declared optimistically.

"Unless they can run as fast as a horse," Blade noted, and slowed to a walk.

Achilles reined up and scowled. "I never thought of that. Some mutants are quite fleet of foot."

"Let's hope these are part turtle," Blade quipped. He

reached the stallion and took the reins from Achilles.

"Surely we can catch them by nightfall."

"We'll do our best," Blade said, and swung onto the black horse. He glanced at the hill, remembering the Flathead's Winchester, and decided against retrieving the rifle. There wasn't time. "Let's go," he directed, and rode to the west.

"Did you find their tracks?" Achilles inquired hopefully.

Blade nodded. "If you're up to it, I don't intend to stop except for nature breaks. No food, no rest until our fellow Warriors and Eagle Feather are safe and sound."

"And Priscilla. Don't forget about her."

"Did I neglect to mention her name?" Blade said, suppressing a grin. "Sorry about that. Now let's ride." He led the way to the wallow, then swung westward. They crossed the field and entered a strip of woods, their eyes riveted to the ground, constantly seeking footprints. Beyond the woods lay a narrow plain, which they traversed in short order. The land began to slope gradually upward, and they found themselves ascending hills thick with pines and fallen timbers. The hills blended into a mountain range.

Three times they found tracks. Once in the comparatively softer soil in a small gully west of the woods. The second set of prints was discovered on the narrow plain. And the last impressions were imbedded in the moist earth next to a trickle of a creek bisecting the hills.

Early on, one fact became readily apparent. The mutations were moving at a swift rate, indicated by the manner in which their footprints were imbedded in the dirt. Because of their weight and their speed, they tended to splatter the mud and earth outward when their feet came down hard.

Blade tried to save time by deducing the probable route taken by the creatures. Most men and animals usually took the path of least resistance; they would go around a mountain instead of over it, or they would skirt dense brush instead of plunging through a thicket. Not so with the Bear People. Blade perceived that the creatures intentionally preferred the most difficult course. Undoubtedly to discourage pursuit, the mutations went directly over hills and mountains and passed through thickets with apparent ease. Either they were incredibly clever or they were amazingly resilient.

Or both.

An hour went by. Then two. Three. By the fourth hour Blade's simmering impatience threatened to shatter his normally superb self-control. He realized catching the things wouldn't be easy, and his anxiety over Hickok and Geronimo mounted. He felt sympathy for Eagle Feather and Priscilla too. But the gunman and the Blackfoot had been his dearest friends since childhood. The three of them had been almost inseparable since the age of four. He knew himself well enough to know that if anything ever happened to them, he'd go crazy with grief. And there wouldn't be a single damn member of the Bear People left alive when he was through.

Well, there wouldn't be, anyway.

By late afternoon they were approaching a narrow pass through the mountains. The shadows were lengthening and the air becoming quite chill.

"We won't find them today," Achilles commented morosely.

"You never know," Blade responded, his tone totally lacking conviction.

"If I ask you a question, will you promise me not to laugh?"

Surprised by the query, Blade looked at the novice. "What's your question?"

"Why is it that all I can think of today is Priscilla? I mean, I hardly know the woman. We talked for a few hours. That's all. And yet I can't seem to get her out of my mind. I keep hearing the silken music of her voice and the cheery sparkle of her laugh. And when I close my eyes, I see every chiseled contour of her radiant beauty. Why?"

"You missed your calling," Blade said, the corners of his mouth curling upward.

"What?"

"You should be a poet."

"I'm serious, Blade."

"And so am I," the giant replied, and sighed. "Do you

want the truth?''

"I would expect nothing less from you."

"You're in love."

Achilles snorted. "I hardly know the woman," he reiterated skeptically.

"Tell that to your hormones."

The man in the red cloak digested the news for half a minute. "Do you feel the same way about Jenny?"

Blade smiled happily. "Yeah. Which astounds me sometimes."

"Why?"

"After all these years, even after having a son, I still love her as much as I did when we were first married," Blade said. He chuckled. "Correction. I love her even more. When a relationship is based in love and nurtured by wisdom, the affection is bound to grow."

"You sound like Plato."

"Who do you think told it to me?"

"I wonder if she feels the same way about me," Achilles remarked.

"I'm afraid I can't help you there. With a woman there's no telling."

"I don't understand."

"Men and women are two distinct varieties of the same species. We're flip sides of the same coin. Although we can love one another and become as close as it's possible for human beings to be, complete comprehension between a man and a woman is impossible. We're essentially different from women, Achilles, and anyone who tells you otherwise doesn't know what he's talking about."

Achilles stared at the giant. "Are those Plato's words?"

"They're mine," Blade said. "Don't get me wrong. I love Jenny with all my heart and soul, and I flatter myself that I know her better than anyone else does. But I still can't predict her every thought and word, and I doubt I'll ever be able to do so. That's part of the mystique of romance."

"What about those who claim that men and women are basically the same except for their sex organs?"

"They're morons. In every part of our being, in our personalities, our minds, and our bodies, we're different from women. Live with one for a while and you'll see what I mean."

"I hope I do, one day."

Blade stared ahead at the pass, a defile averaging ten yards in width and 20 feet in height, its walls composed of smooth, solid rock. He leaned forward and peered at the soil, seeking tracks. He entered the pass first, engrossed in scrutinizing the dirt, wondering if the Bear People would continue to the west on the opposite side of the mountain range. He was grateful the creatures were in such a hurry. Otherwise, he'd have to worry about the possibility of an ambush.

As it turned out, he should have worried anyway.

Blade realized his error the next moment when he heard a feral snarl from overhead and glanced up in time to see a bestial form hurtling toward him.

CHAPTER SIXTEEN

The sun was just rising above the eastern horizon when Hickok obtained his first clear look at his abductors. He'd been carried for hours, the creatures covering mile after mile, over hills and mountains and along a winding valley, and he'd expected them to keep going during the day. At dawn, however, they moved into a stand of trees until they arrived at a spacious clearing, and the next thing Hickok knew, he was being unceremoniously deposited on the ground. He landed on his back, grunting from the discomfort, and glanced around.

Geronimo, Eagle Feather, Priscilla Wendling, and another woman were being dumped to the turf a few feet away.

Hickok stared at the creatures doing the dumping, the short hairs at the base of his neck prickling. He automatically reached for his Colts, groping from holster to holster, forgetting the guns were gone.

The Bear People, as the Flatheads referred to the mutations, did indeed possess an unnatural combination of human and bearlike traits. There were 37 of the creatures walking around, all adults, the majority males. They stood between six and six and a half feet tall and weighed in the neighborhood of 210 pounds. Their shoulders were wide, their bodies endowed with rippling muscles, their legs perpetually bowlegged, and they walked with an odd, stooped-over posture. Bedraggled black hair hung to their shoulders and covered their shoulders, upper arms, abdomens, and legs. In contrast, their faces and upper chest were pale and hairless.

And what visages! Low, sloping foreheads were rimmed by beetle brows that protruded above dark eyes. The nostrils were long and rounded, much like the nostrils on bears, and their cheeks were concave. Pointed teeth glistened when they opened their thick-lipped mouths.

Other than deer-hide loinclothes and skimpy tops covering the pendulous breasts of the females, they were naked.

Hickok struggled to a sitting position and glanced at his companions.

Geronimo was also sitting up. Priscilla lay on her right side, gawking at the mutations. Eagle Feather was intently scanning the clearing. The other woman, a brunette wearing beige slacks and a green blouse, had fallen to her knees and appeared to be too terrified to move.

The gunfighter focused on his best friend. "Well, this is another fine mess you've gotten me into."

"Me?" Geronimo responded. "What did I do?"

"You dozed off on guard duty and let these critters conk you on the noggin'."

"I was wide awake, I'll have you know."

Hickok grinned. "Oh, really? And what happened to those great Injun senses and reflexes I keep hearin' about?"

"They took me by surprise," Geronimo said lamely while testing the leather thongs binding his wrists.

"I recollect you tellin' me that no one can sneak up on an Indian," Hickok said, and smirked.

"You misunderstood."

"I did?"

"Yeah. I meant no white man."

"Is that a fact? At least I got off a few shots. What did

you do? Breathe on them?''

Priscilla leaned toward them, glaring. "How can you two joke at a time like this?'' she demanded angrily. "We've been captured by mutants!''

"No foolin'?'' Hickok responded.

"Where are they?'' Eagle Feather interjected.

"Who?'' the gunfighter asked.

"My wife and sons. I don't see them,'' Eagle Feather stated, his emotional anguish transparent.

"The creatures might have your family elsewhere,'' Geronimo said.

"I pray they do,'' Eagle Feather said.

Priscilla pulled her knees up to her chest, then rolled onto her shins. "You've got to get us out of here,'' she told the gunman.

Hickok snickered. "Yeah. Right. I'll sprout wings and fly all of us out.''

"There must be something you can do!''

A brittle laugh came from off to the left. "There's nothing any of you can do,'' a surly voice declared. "The sooner you accept your fate, the better.''

Hickok twisted, his eyes narrowing.

Three of the creatures were strolling toward the captives. The mutation in the lead, the tallest of them all, bore a jagged scar on the right side of his face, from the corner of his eyes to the tip of his pronounced chin. The scar distinguished him from his comrades, and so did the tomahawk he clutched in his huge right hand. His fingernails, like all those of the Bear People, were over an inch long and slightly curved.

"Talkin' bears,'' Hickok quipped. "Now I've seen everything.''

The trio halted, and the apparent leader placed his hands on his stout hips and glowered at the gunfighter.

"My name is Longat. I'm the head of the Breed.''

"My condolences,'' Hickok cracked.

"Have your fun while you can,'' the creature named Longat stated. "We'll save you for last so we can watch you suffer.''

"What are you?" Priscilla asked. "Why have you done this to us?"

Longat glanced at the creature on the left and grinned. "Humans, eh?"

"They're pathetic," growled the second mutation.

"If I had my Colts I'd show you pathetic, you turkey," Hickok stated.

"What's your name?" Longat queried.

"Hickok."

"Keep flapping your gums, Hickok, and I'll gut you right here," Longat vowed, and looked at the Mormon woman. "Can't you figure out what we are?"

"You're mutations."

"How perceptive," Longat said.

All three creatures laughed.

"What do you intend to do with us?" Priscilla asked.

"Do you really want to know?"

"Yes."

Longat grinned, a malevolent expression devoid of mirth. "I'd rather keep you in suspense. It's more fun that way."

"Where are you from?" Hickok asked.

"Wouldn't you like to know?" the mutation retorted.

Eagle Feather bent toward the leader. "Where's my family? What have you done with my wife and sons?"

"Your family?" Longat repeated quizzically. He studied the Flathead for a bit, then nodded. "I remember you. You're the one we almost crushed in the rock slide. You're the husband of Morning Dew and those two brats."

Fury contorted the Flathead's countenance and he endeavored to rise, pushing upward with his tied hands. His injured left thigh, stiff and sore after so many hours of being held still, buckled and he fell onto his hands and elbows.

"Your concern for your loved ones is touching," Longat stated, his words reeking with contempt.

"Where are they?" Eagle Feather shouted, crimson flushing his features.

"Have a care, human. Control yourself or you'll never learn their whereabouts."

Eagle Feather rose on his knees, heedless of the warning. "Where are my wife and sons?" he shouted.

Like a striking rattler, displaying astounding speed, Longat swiftly stepped forward and backhanded the Flathead across the mouth, knocking Eagle Feather onto the grass. "Fool! *We* are the masters here. Mouth off again and I'll take you next."

Glaring up at the mutation, Eagle Feather wiped the back of his hands over his cracked, bloody lips.

"Take him where?" Hickok asked.

"Nowhere."

"But you just said—" Hickok began.

"I know what I said," Longat snapped. "And you'll comprehend the truth soon enough."

"I can hardly wait."

The head of the Breed looked at the timid brunette. "What's your name?" he demanded.

The woman stared blankly at the creature but did not utter a sound.

"Didn't you hear me?" Longat said. "What's your name?"

"It's Milly Odum," Priscilla answered. "Can't you see that she's too scared to think straight? Why don't you leave her alone?"

Longat took a pace and grabbed Odum by the hair. She winced and cowered, trembling uncontrollably. "Yes. You're healthy. You'll do."

"What are you going to do with her?" Priscilla questioned, irate at Odum's treatment. "She hasn't done anything to you."

"And she never will," Longat stated. He released Odum and started to stalk off with the other two creatures in tow.

"Hold it!" Geronimo finally spoke up.

Longat halted and glanced back. "What now, human?"

"That's *my* tomahawk you're carrying."

"Really?" Longat hefted the weapon, admiring the crafts-manship. "And I neglected to thank you for your gift. How careless." He laughed and walked away.

"I can't wait to plug that hombre," Hickok commented.

"You'll have to wait your turn," Geronimo said.

Priscilla glanced from Warrior to Warrior. "What's our next move? How can we escape from these monsters?"

"Beats me," Hickok replied.

"You're supposed to be the expert," Priscilla stated. "Is that all you can say?"

"For the time being."

"Some tough guy you are."

"What do you want from me, lady? The leather holdin' our wrists is too strong to break. And even if I could, what chance would I have against all these critters when I'm unarmed?"

"Hey, look," Geronimo said, and nodded at the opposite side of the clearing.

Hickok swung around.

The mutations had placed three of their own, all evidently dead, near the far trees. All three were lying on their backs with their hands neatly folded on their stomachs.

"I didn't realize I killed so many," Hickok said.

"How do you know that you were responsible?" Geronimo inquired.

"It certainly wasn't you, pard. You were in dreamland, as I recollect."

"Rub it in, why don't you?"

"Gladly."

Priscilla made a hissing noise. "You two are so exasperating! Here we are in the clutches of a pack of freaks, and all you two can do is bicker."

"If you have a plan, I'd love to hear it," Hickok said.

"Yeah," Geronimo chimed in. "We're all ears."

"I don't have one at the moment."

"I figured as much," Hickok stated. "When you do, then you can criticize us."

"You're impossible!" Priscilla declared.

"That's what my missus keeps sayin'," Hickok observed. He surveyed the clearing, noting sentries had been posted at 20-foot intervals around the perimeter. Although he wanted to escape just as badly as Priscilla, what else could he do? For the time being he was stuck where they were.

"I'll just have to wait for Achilles to come and save us," Priscilla said.

"You're partial to that whippersnapper, aren't you?" Hickok said.

"None of your damn business."

"Yep. You are."

"Are you a mind reader?" Priscilla asked sarcastically.

"Nope. But I do know that when a woman acts contrary, she usually is hidin' something."

"My. I never would have guessed you're a student a human nature."

"And I don't know why you're pickin' on me when there are heaps of real lowlifes you can vent your spleen on."

Priscilla opened her mouth to speak, then changed her mind and averted her face. "I'm sorry. It's just that I'm terrified of what will happen to us. I don't mean to take it out on you."

"That's okay. I'm married."

"So?"

"So I'm used to havin' a female dump on me all the time."

"You're incorrigible."

"I am?" Hickok responded, and beamed. "Thanks." He glanced at Geronimo. "I bet nobody ever pays you compliments like that."

"You've got me there."

Eagle Feather suddenly sat up, scowling. "This is insane! Here we are, about to die, and you act as if you don't have a care in the world!"

"Calm down," Hickok advised. "Gettin' all bent all of shape won't help us a bit. Why do you think we're makin' light of the situation? Because we're crazy? We do it to keep our sanity intact, to get a handle on things until we can make our break. If you brood on it, you'll go to pieces."

"Warriors must take courses in combat psychology taught by an experienced Elder," Geronimo disclosed. "We're trained to control our reactions to brutality and danger by trying to take everything in stride. We're affected by all of this, just like you, only we learned a long time ago to take what comes as calmly as possible. Humor is just one of the tools we use. Otherwise, we couldn't stand the strain.''

"I could never be a Warrior," Eagle Feather said.

"You never know until you try," Hickok said. He saw a trio of familiar figures coming toward them. "Uh-oh. Here comes Gruesome again.''

Longat and the two creatures with him approached to within a yard of the prisoners, then halted.

"Forget something?" Hickok quipped.

"No," Longat replied, and nodded at the pair beside him. They immediately walked to Milly Odum and roughly hauled her to her feet.

"What are you planning to do with her?" Priscilla asked. "Leave her alone!''

"Yeah!" Hickok stated. "What's she to you?''

A scornful smile creased Longat's countenance. "Breakfast.''

CHAPTER SEVENTEEN

Blade felt strong hands clamp on his shoulders as a heavy body struck him squarely in the chest, and the next instant he was flying from the saddle with the creature on top of him. He twisted to the right as he fell, hoping to dislodge his hairy attacker. They both crashed onto the rocky ground with a bone-jarring impact.

The thing snarled and lunged at the Warrior's throat.

A repulsive image of hair and teeth and hate-filled eyes loomed inches from Blade's face. Sharp nails bit into his neck, and before they could rip his throat apart he grabbed the creature's wrists and strained, pulling its hands loose.

The booming of Achilles' Bullpup reverberated in the stony defile.

Blade heaved, shoving the mutation from him, and swept to his feet. A hasty glance showed three of the creatures converging on Achilles, but there was nothing he could do to assist the novice. The thing that had pounced on him was erect, and there were two others charging him, their clawed fingers extended to tear into him.

Damn.

He'd waltzed right into their trap.

Although the Henry was slung over his left arm and the Commando over his right, and even though he had the Pythons jammed under his belt, Blade's hands flashed to the weapons he preferred the most, the knives he had wielded ever since he was old enough to hold them. The Bowies speared up and out just as the first creature leaped at him.

The mutation threw back its head and vented a strident screech as the blades sank to their hilts in its chest.

Blade wrenched the Bowies downward, slicing the creature open all the way to the abdomen. Then he wrenched the knives sideways, tugged them out, and spun.

Too late.

One of the Bear People closed in from either side. Each took hold of a brawny arm and held fast, apparently intending to capture the Warrior alive.

Blade whipped his body forward, causing the creatures to lose their balance, and quickly, savagely reversed direction. His tactic succeeded. The two mutations lost their footing and stumbled, their grips slackening. With a herculean effort, every muscle of his arms and shoulders bulging, Blade tore his arms from their grasp, causing the Henry to fall to the ground in the process.

His respite was short-lived.

The thing on the right swiped its claws at the giant's eyes.

Ducking, Blade narrowly missed having his pupils punctured. He pivoted and lanced the Bowies into the creature's exposed jugular, and he blinked when blood sprayed onto his forehead and cheeks. To nail the mutation on the right he'd been forced to turn his back on the one on the left, and now a grimy arm encircled his neck from the rear and squeezed.

Blade released the Bowies and tottered backwards as intense pressure threatened to crush his trachea. He frantically drove his right elbow around in a tight arc and connected with the creature's ribs, but the pressure only increased. He reached up, seized the arm squeezing him, and executed a flawless jujitsu throw, dropping onto his right knee and flipping the mutation onto the ground. The Commando clattered at his feet.

He had no time to grab it.

The creature he'd stabbed in the throat had pulled the knives free. A crimson spray gushing from his neck, the thing hissed, raised the Bowies overhead for a downward thrust, and sprang.

In a lightning insight, Blade perceived that he'd discovered the key to defeating his foes. They were fierce brutes who relied on their strength and speed; they knew nothing of the martial arts. To win, he had to take the offensive and employ every martial skill he knew. No sooner did the thought flicker through his mind than he placed his palms on the ground and performed a full circle sweep, his left leg rigid. He caught the creature behind the knees and the thing slammed onto its back.

But the other two were already up.

Blade straightened, staring in astonishment at the mutation he'd gutted. Intestines and gore were oozing from the cuts, and still the thing was coming at him.

What did it take to kill them?

The Warrior went for the weakest creature first, for the one with the intestines hanging out. He leaped into the air and delivered a spinning back kick. His foot struck the mutation in the head and bowled the creature over.

The third mutation charged as the giant landed.

Blade barely had time to react. The thing rammed him in the stomach and looped its arms around his waist, upending him, and he rolled with the momentum, falling onto his buttocks and arching his back while driving his left knee into the creature's midriff. He succeeded in tossing his bestial adversary over his head, then rolled to the left and rose, drawing the Pythons.

So much for the martial arts.

The things could fight all day, if need be, even when severely injured. He needed to end the battle, and end it now.

At point-blank range Blade shot the one creature he hadn't knifed in the head, then whirled and planted two slugs in the brain of the brute with the ravaged throat.

Leaving Gutsy.

Blade pointed both barrels at the mutation as it stood unsteadily. "Don't make me shoot," he warned.

The thing glanced at the Warrior and grinned, a chilling gesture of defiance. "Screw you, human!"

For a moment Blade was stupefied. He'd never anticipated that the thing could *talk*! Stunned, he was sluggish to respond when the creature roared and shuffled toward him. It almost reached him before he squeezed the trigger on the right Colt, intentionally aiming low.

Growling and lashing out with its tapered nails, the mutation collapsed when the slug tore through its left knee. It fell onto its left side, its inner organs still seeping from the gaping slashes.

"Drop the guns, human!"

Blade whirled at the command, the Pythons level in his hand.

Two of the three Bear People who had attacked Achilles were dead, their craniums blown to bits by the Bullpup. The Mossberg lay on the ground between the pair.

The third creature had its left arm encircling Achilles' neck. In its right hand, the barrel touching the novice's temple, was the Taurus. "I won't tell you again!" the mutation snapped. "Just because we seldom use human weapons, don't think I can't use this." He gouged the Taurus into Achilles. "Now drop those damn guns or your friend is wolf bait."

Blade hesitated. If he possessed Hickok's skill, he'd be tempted to shoot the bear-man before it knew what happened. But his expertise, the skill to which he had devoted almost all of his life, lay in the consummate use of edged weapons. Frowning, he started to lower the Colts.

Achilles appeared to be in a bind. With the mutation holding him from behind, there didn't seem to be much he could do. His left hand gripped the arm that held him. He could feel the Taurus digging into his skin, and he saw Blade reluctantly comply. His right hand disappeared under the folds of his red cloak.

"That's it," the creature said, watching the Pythons droop toward the ground. "Smart move, for a human."

"What are you?" Blade asked, hoping to distract the mutation. He'd seen Achilles' right hand vanish and he guessed what would happen next.

"My name is Nuprix. I belong to the Breed."

"Strange name," Blade commented, stalling, continuing to slowly lower the Pythons to the ground instead of simply dropping them.

The creature watched the Colts, concentrating on the revolvers to the exclusion of all else. "Most of the Breed stopped using typical human names decades ago."

"Why's that?"

"Just put those damn guns down and shut up!" Nuprix barked.

Blade squatted and eased the revolvers to within six inches of the dirt. He surmised that Achilles would make a move soon, that the novice hadn't budged a muscle to give the mutation the false impression of having given up. His conjecture proved accurate.

The Amazon suddenly flashed out from under the red cloak as Achilles swept the big knife up and angled the gleaming blade straight back above his head. The tip sliced into the creature's right cheek, then penetrated its right eye, puncturing the orb and sinking deep.

Nuprix bellowed and staggered to the left, releasing Achilles and tearing loose from the imbedded knife. The mutation clutched at its ruined eye, then howled and pointed the Taurus at the blond man.

Blade elevated the Pythons and snapped off two hasty shots. The bullets hit Nuprix in the chest and rocked the creature on its heels. Quickly Blade aimed carefully, sighting on the thing's forehead, and squeezed both triggers.

Straightening, Blade glanced at Achilles. "Nice move. I couldn't have done better myself."

"Thanks," Achilles responded, and glanced past the head Warrior. "Look out!"

Blade whirled, astounded to discover the last mutation three feet away, persistently striving to reach him with its nails. Despite being shot in the left knee, and despite the fact its intestines were dangling from its ruptured abdomen, the thing had risen on its right leg and was shuffling forward. "Stop!" Blade commanded.

The creature snarled and lunged.

Taking a stride backwards to evade the mutation's nails, Blade pointed the left Python at the mutation's right knee and fired.

Again the bearish figure crumpled, gritting its teeth against the pain, and glared up at the giant. "Finish me!"

"Not yet," Blade said.

The creature motioned at its split adominal wall. "Damn you, human! Look at me! Do the honorable deed and finish me off!"

"What would you know about honor?"

"Up yours."

Blade cautiously skirted the mutation, tucked the Colts under his belt once more, and swiftly reclaimed his Bowies, wiping the blades clean on his fatigue pants. He returned to the creature. "So you want me to put you out of your misery?"

"That's the general idea, bastard."

"I'll do it if you'll answer a few questions."

"Get stuffed," the thing said, and grunted in agony.

"Suit yourself, stupid," Blade said, baiting the Breed.

Achilles came over, the Amazon back in its sheath, the Bullpup in his hands.

A groan issued from the mutation's lips and it doubled over, racked by torment.

"If you want to suffer, that's fine with me," Blade said. "But what harm could a few questions do?"

The thing glanced up, crimson spittle flecking its mouth. "What do you want to know?"

"What's your name?"

"Yeddt."

"Why did you attack us?"

"Longat gave us orders to watch our back trail, and to capture any scuzzy humans who showed up."

"Longat is the leader of the Breed?"

"Yes," Yeddt stated. He closed his eyes and inhaled raggedly.

Blade squatted, his Bowies held at the ready. "Tell me about the Breed. Why do you call yourself by that name? Where are you from?"

Yeddt said nothing.

"Come on," Blade prompted. "If you want to linger in misery for hours, that's your business. I'll only finish you if you cooperate." He paused, striving to come up with a persuasive argument. "I certainly couldn't use any information you supply against your people, could I?"

The mutation opened its eyes and stared at the Warrior. "No, I guess not."

"Then answer my questions and end your torture."

Yeddt licked his lips and coughed. "I don't have much choice. All right. But I won't tell you the exact location of our base of operations no matter what."

"Fair enough."

"It all started about a decade after the war," Yeddt revealed, speaking softly, blood trickling from the right corner of his mouth. "During World War Three a bunch of survivalists hid out in the mountains, in a secluded valley where there was plenty of game and a large lake. The survivalists built cabins and lived off the land, and they stayed there after the war was over because there was nothing to return to."

Blade listened attentively, breathing shallowly, almost nauseated by the sickening odor arising from the mutation's intestines and abdominal cavity.

"About ten years after the war the changes started," Yeddt said, and coughed again.

"Changes?"

"Yeah. The survivalists began to change, to become hairier and heavier. And their babies were even more different. No one could figure out what was going on. They thought the radiation might be to blame," Yeddt related, then trembled briefly. "Later they found the canisters."

"What canisters?" Blade probed.

"About a dozen metal canisters were found in the lake. Biological-warfare canisters."

Blade stiffened. "How did the canisters get in the lake?"

"No one could figure that out, either, until the hermit told them about the plane."

"Who was this hermit?"

"An old geezer who lived all by himself way up in the mountains. He came down to trade with the survivalists every now and then, and he told them about this plane that had been flying real low over the mountains one night a month after the war started. He'd seen this plane, a bomber he thought it was, circling as if looking for a place to land. Smoke was coming from one of its engines. The bomber went over a ridge to the west and never came back, and the old man didn't think much of it," Yeddt said. "A few days later, the survivalists showed up."

Blade mentally filled in the missing pieces of the puzzle. The bomber must have been carrying biological weapons and either taken a hit or developed engine trouble. Too far from the nearest base, and probably losing altitude, the pilot undoubtedly decided to ditch the aircraft. But before taking the bomber down, the crew apparently opted to dump their load of biological weapons somewhere relatively safe, away from inhabited settlements. And what would have been safer, in their point of view, than an isolated lake in a remote valley? So they'd released the canisters into the water and later crashed. Maybe every crew member was killed. In any event, no one ever returned for the canisters.

A few days later the survivalists moved into the valley and used the lake as their source of drinking and bathing water. Unknown to them, some of the canisters had sprung leaks and contaminated the lake with biological toxins. So after a decade of consuming the tainted water, after the chemicals permeated their systems and warped their glands, the survivalists began to change into something other than human. The poor, vulnerable embryos in their mothers' wombs were especially susceptible to the gene-altering effects of the compounds.

Dear Spirit!

What a horrid fate!

"Eventually everyone became as you are," Blade stated. "A bearish mutation."

Yeddt nodded.

"Why didn't the survivalists just move out of the valley? They might have been able to reverse the effects."

"Some tried. But when they left the valley, they were killed by people who feared them for no other reason than their appearance. The rest realized they could never leave. They weren't about to abandon the children already born. And they couldn't mingle with their former fellow humans. So they stayed and multiplied."

"And decided to call themselves the Breed?"

"Yes. They considered themselves a breed apart from humans. The name fits, don't you think?"

Blade nodded.

"Over the years the Breed have grown in numbers, and now we fill our valley. Our leader, Longat, decided to send an expedition into the outside world, to test the humans, to see if we can spread outward and control more territory."

"But why do you hate humans so much? You were humans once."

"No, I wasn't!" Yeddt declared with surprising strength. "My great-great-grandparents were humans. But I was born as you see me now. I was born special. One of the Breed."

"That still doesn't explain why you hate us."

Yeddt leaned toward the giant, malice radiating from his feral eyes. "Because your kind hates us! Humans despise our kind. They kill us every chance they get. The inhabitants of the town twenty miles from our valley once sent an armed posse to wipe us out." He smiled. "We taught them a lesson!"

"What did you do?" Blade asked.

The creature smacked its lips. "Yummy."

Blade glanced at Achilles, then at the mutation. "Are you telling me you ate them?"

"Wouldn't you like to know!"

"The Breed are cannibals?" Blade declared, aghast at the prospect.

"Cannibals are those who eat their own kind," Yeddt stated arrogantly. "Humans aren't our kind."

"But surely the Breed don't eat humans?"

"And why not? Human meat is the tastiest there is, even better than buffalo steak."

"You're disgusting!" Achilles interjected.

"Are we, swine? Let me give you some advice. You take what you can get in this life, and only the strong survive. About sixty years ago the worst winter in Idaho history had the Breed boxed in. Twenty-foot drifts blocked the passes to the lowlands. The game was scarce and hard to catch, so the Breed turned to another food source to stay alive."

"They took to eating humans," Blade said distastefully.

Yeddt grinned and nodded. "There were a lot of humans living in the mountains surrounding our valley back then. This was before we declared war on humanity. That winter, when there was no other food to be had, the Breed turned to the only other source of nourishment available."

Blade thought of Hickok, Geronimo, and the others. "Do the Breed still eat humans?"

"What a dumb question. Of course."

"Are our friends still alive? Have they been eaten?"

"That's for me to know and you to find out."

"What about the woman you captured?" Achilles queried.

"Which one?"

"The Breed captured more than one?" Achilles responded puzzled.

"They must have Milly Odum," Blade conjectured.

Achilles took a step nearer the mutation. "Where are they?"

"I'll never tell."

"We need to know," Blade said.

"Tough."

"Do you want your torment to end or not?" Blade asked.

Yeddt stared at the giant. "You promised."

"Only if you answered all of my questions."

"I can't tell you were they're at."

"Then do the next best thing. Tell me the direction the Breed are taking? Tell me where they're heading?"

"I can't."

"Then suffer."

Yeddt hissed. "I should have known you wouldn't keep your word. All humans are alike!"

"In one respect you're right," Blade stated. "We stick together when the going gets rough. For the last time, which way are the Breed heading?"

"Go play with yourself."

Blade had anticipated such a reply and he instantaneously reacted, surging forward and arcing his right Bowie down and in, lancing the tip into Yeddt's groin.

The mutation screamed and tried to cover its genitals while sliding backwards.

Jerking the knife out, Blade wagged the weapon in front of the creature's nose, splattering blood on its face. "I won't ask you again. If you don't answer, I guarantee you that your suffering will just be beginning. By the time I'm done, you'll be begging for mercy."

"You son of a bitch!" Yeddt cried, hands over his groin, blood dripping between his legs, a scarlet stain discoloring his loincloth.

"I gave you your chance," Blade said, and made a movement as it to stab the creature again.

"Hold it!" Yeddt declared.

"I'm listening."

A low whine issued from Yeddt's throat. He stared at his loincloth and shuddered. "You'd make a good Breed."

"Don't change the subject."

"All right. I'll tell you where they're headed. Not that the information will do you any good. Even you can't prevail against Longat and the others."

"Where?" Blade demanded harshly.

Yeddt told them.

"Thanks," Blade said. He stood, slipped the Bowies into thier sheaths, and looked at Achilles. "I'd like to borrow your Bullpup for a minute."

"Be my guest," the novice responded, and handed the weapon over.

Blaze gazed at the mutation. "Close your eyes and open your mouth."

Yeddt obeyed.

"Wider."

The mutation opened its mouth as wide as it could.

Without displaying a flicker of emotion, Blade inserted the shotgun barrel between the creature's lips and squeezed the trigger.

CHAPTER EIGHTEEN

Hickok sprang erect, as did the rest of his companions, and took a stride toward the leader of the Breed. "Get your paws off her!" he snapped.

"What do you mean by breakfast?" Priscilla queried, watching the pair of bearish mutations start to convey Milly Odum to the center of the clearing.

"Surely a smart human like you can figure it out," Longat replied, and turned.

Eagle Feather's features registered profound shock. He ran up behind Longat, grabbed the creature by the left shoulder, and spun the genetic deviate around. "You didn't!"

Longat's visage became a mask of sheer hatred. "You dare lay a hand on me, you human scum!" he bellowed, and raised the tomahawk overhead.

With a swift bound Hickok launched himself into the air and tackled Eagle Feather, looping his arms around the Flathead's waist and bearing both of them to the ground before the mutation could strike. He let go and rolled to his feet.

Over a dozen of the Breed converged on the captives,

surrounding the humans to prevent them from interfering.

Glowering, Longat slowly lowered the tomahawk. "You were lucky this time," he said to the Flathead. "I don't want to waste food. But we'll take you next." He wheeled and stalked off.

"What does he mean by food?" Priscilla inquired of no one in particular. "He can't mean what I think he means."

"He does," Hickok confirmed, and offered his hand to Eagle Feather.

"You saved my life," the Flathead said, and allowed the gunfighter to pull him up.

"Think nothin' of it."

"I wish you hadn't."

"Why?"

Eagle Feather gazed toward the middle of the clearing, where the rest of the Breed were forming a circle around Milly Odum. "Because now I know what happened to my family. I wish I was dead."

"Would your loved ones want you to give up without a fight?" Hickok asked, noticing the sorrow etching lines in the Flathead's face.

Eagle Feather appeared not to hear the question. He looked blankly down at the grass. "My wife and sons are gone," he said softly, stunned. "And what a horrible way to go."

"Don't you want to get revenge?" Hickok commented.

Again the Flathead did not respond. "Those I loved most have been taken from me! Murdered by these monsters!"

Geronimo placed his bound hands on Eagle Feather's right shoulder. "I know how rough this is for you. We're here if you need us."

"I'm too late," Eagle Feather said numbly. "Too late."

"What are they doing to Milly?" Priscilla interjected.

The petrified woman was standing with her arms hanging limp and utter helplessness reflected in her expression, gaping at the ring of hostile creatures surrounding her. Her lower lip trembled and her fingers twitched.

"We've got to help her!" Priscilla declared.

Hickok scanned the 14 mutations enclosing them. "How?"

"I don't know. But there must be something we can do."

One of the Breed laughed. "There's nothing you can do, human. Watch closely, because it will be your turn before you know it."

His stomach tightening into a knot, Hickok saw Longat weave through the pack of abominations and walk directly up to Odum. The woman gazed fearfully into the mutation's eyes.

"Oh God. No!" Priscilla said. "Please no!"

Four of the Breed detached themselves from the main group and hurried into the forest, returning within a minute bearing limbs and sticks which they carried to the middle and deposited near Longat and Odum. They made another trip to gather wood, and came back with even more.

"That should be enough," Longat told them, and nodded at the pair who usually attended him.

The duo seized Odum by the arms and held her fast.

"Brothers and sisters of the Breed," Longat said, raising his arms and beaming. "The time has come for us to feed again. Because we've been fortunate enough to obtain a supply of our favorite delicacy, we'll enjoy a feast and remain here until noon. But before we fill our bellies, I must address you on an important issue."

"How soon before we return to our valley?" a husky male interrupted.

"We'll be home in two weeks," Longat stated. "We've seen enough of the outside world to know that the humans will pose no serious threat to our plans to expand the territory under our control. We'll start slowly at first and subjugate those towns nearest to our valley. In ten years we should control all of the former state of Idaho."

Hickok couldn't resist the opportunity to taunt the mutation. He cupped his hands to his mouth and shouted, "You're out of your gourd, jerk-face. There aren't enough of your bozos to take over a whole blamed state."

Longat stared balefully at the Warrior. "There will be once we convert half of the humans we capture."

"Convert them to what? Your slaves?"

"No, you pathetic imbecile. We have the means of transforming humans into the genetically superior species we are."

The revelation jolted Hickok. For a few seconds he believed that Longat might be lying to get his goat, until he saw the leader's smug countenance. "That's impossible," he blurted out.

"You wish it was impossible. But we can transform hundreds, even thousands of lowly humans given time and their unwitting cooperating."

"How?"

"We have a way."

"You'll never get the time you need," Hickok said. "The Federation will send in an army to eliminate every last one of you."

"We know about the Federation. And we know the Federation can't destroy us without first locating our home, which they'll never do. There's no way the Federation army can cover every square inch of the Pacific Northwest."

"The Federation will stop you crumbs," Hickok stated, hoping he projected more confidence than he felt.

Longat gave a contemptuous wave of his hand, dismissing the statement as irrelevant, and faced his followers. "You've heard this human babble, and you all know how insignificant humans are in the grand scheme of things. Back in the early days, when the Breed initially appeared, there were those of our ancestors who viewed the transformation as a curse. They were still new to their condition and foolishly persisted in regarding humans as the acme of development on his planet." He paused and smirked. "But we know better now. We know that humans are a blight, a demented species who nearly obliterated all life on Earth. They have no natural right to rule this world. They lost any claim to ascendancy by conclusively demonstrating their inherent insanity."

"Humans suck!" one of the creatures yelled.

"Death to all human scum!" chimed in another.

"No, not to all of them," Longat corrected him. "We'll cultivate some of the humans as a food source, but our primary priority must be to increase our own ranks, to render us invincible. That is the reason I've proposed using the lake water to transmute large numbers of humans. Between natural reproduction of our species and the transformation process, we can triple our population in a single generation. In two generations the Breed will number over one hundred thousand and the humans will crumble before our combined might.''

Lake water? What did lake water have to do with the transformation? Hickok wondered. He stared at Milly Odum, at her terrified face, his heart going out to her, wishing he could save her from her impending fate. But what could he do with his wrists tied? He glanced down at his hands, furious at his vincibility.

"Long live the Breed!" Longat cried.

From the throats of every creature came the same cry, repeated in unison several times. "Long live the Breed! Long live the Breed! Long live the Breed!"

Hickok looked at the mutation standing in front of him and smiled sweetly. "I hope you all keel over by tomorrow."

"And now to enjoy our feast!" Longat declared, turning to Odum. "Prepare her!"

The duo who always attended the leader stepped in close and snatched at the woman's clothes, easily tearing the fabric with their nails, laughing evilly as they stripped her naked.

Odum screeched and vainly tried to cover herself with her hands, tears streaming from the corners of her eyes.

Many of the Breed cackled at her discomfiture.

Geronimo, scowling, looked at the gunfighter. "We can't just stand here and let them kill her."

"I know, pard."

"Then when?"

"Now," Hickok said, and leaped at the nearest mutation, his hands clenched together, sweeping his arms up and then lashing out at the creature's head.

Geronimo jumped at another bear-man.

For a few moments the Warriors had the advantage of surprise and the mutations briefly gave way.

Hickok smashed his knuckles into the mouth of the closest creature, knocking it backwards, and then swung at the mutation on his right, clipping the thing on the side of the head and knocking it down.

Geronimo succeeded in battering two of the bear-men to the ground and managed to take four swift strides in the direction of Milly Odum.

The remaining guards pounced en masse, swarming over the Warriors and overwhelming them by sheer force of numbers.

Heavy fists thudded into Hickok's face and stomach, and he doubled over. He beat at the Breed ineffectually. There were simply too many. Hands roughly seized his arms and one of the bear-men applied a headlock. He glimpsed Geronimo being similarly subdued and ceased to resist. The things were holding him in viselike grips and he couldn't move his arms or legs.

"Be still, human!" a burly brute hissed, and slapped the gunman across the mouth.

The salty taste of blood touched Hickok's tongue, and he glared at the creature that had struck him. "You'll get yours, sucker!"

"Fat chance."

Hickok twisted his head to see the middle of the clearing. Longat and the majority of the Breed had been intently watching the one-sided struggle. Now Longat chuckled and nodded at the duo.

"Hold her arms!"

Milly screamed and attempted to pull free as the hairy beast men took hold of her, each one clasping a wrist and extending her arm to its limit.

"Leave her alone!" Priscilla shouted, tears in her own eyes, her slim hands molded into fists.

Longat ignored the distraction. He hefted the tomahawk and stepped in front of the helpless prisoner. "Have you any last words, woman?"

Milly's eyes were as wide as they could be. Her mouth moved but no words came out.

''Articulate bitch, aren't you?'' Longat quipped.

Hickok vented a growling noise every bit as bestial as the bear-men could make. A burning rage flared in every cell of his being. Never had he felt so frustrated! He glanced at Eagle Feather, who was standing a few feet away, seemingly in a daze, then back at the tableau in the center of the clearing.

Longat was smiling broadly. ''Let us proceed,'' he said, and nodded again.

The two creatures grasping Odum's arms suddenly surged in opposite directions, every muscle on their bodies rippling, as they pulled with all their might.

Milly lifted her face to the sky and gave voice to a plaintive wail.

Hickok grit his teeth in impotent fury. He saw the duo strain, exerting their enormous strength, and he saw Milly Odum shriek in abject fear, and then her arms parted from her shoulders with a sickening ripping sound, tendrils of flesh hanging from the ragged sockets, blood spurting from each cavity.

Milly's eyelids fluttered and she started to collapse.

Gleaming in the sunlight, the tomahawk whipped in an arc as Longat buried the edge in her forehead, cleaving her skull nearly in half, exposing her brain. He laughed as he wrenched the weapon loose.

Dead on her feet, Milly Odum's body sank slowly to the ground.

The duo waved the severed arms they had held in the air, beaming happily.

Hickok felt flushed. He wanted to pound every last one of the Breed into a pulp. A bitter bile rose in his mouth and he swallowed it. A frenzied cry to his left drew his attention to Priscilla.

The Mormon woman had taken all she could stand. Her self-control snapped and she threw herself recklessly at a nearby bear-man, striking at its face, tears streaming down her cheeks.

Startled, the mutation defended itself instinctively, lashing out with a malletlike hand. His blow caught Priscilla on the tip of her chin and snapped her head back with an audible crack.

"No!" Hickok yelled, striving to break free.

Priscilla Wendling straightened, her forehead knit in bewilderment. She endeavored to speak, but her head sagged to the right at an unnatural angle and she abruptly pitched forward.

"No! No!" Hickok shouted, tugging and thrashing.

Priscilla lay on the grass, her head tilted crazily upward, her lifeless eyes fixed on eternity.

Hickok went slack, staring at her in shock.

"Let me through!"

The creatures parted at the command and Longat walked up to the Mormon woman and halted. The bloody tomahawk was in his right hand. He frowned and looked around. "Who did this?"

"I did," replied the mutation responsible. "I'm sorry," he added sheepishly.

"You idiot, Komsey!" Longat barked. "You know that wasting meat is strictly forbidden."

"She took me by surprise," Komsey responded. "I didn't mean to hit her so hard."

Longat sighed and placed his hands on his hips. "Well, it's no use crying over spilt blood. And we're not going to let her go to waste. Get the fire going. We'll eat both of them." He smiled. "There's nothing like a hearty meal and a full stomach after a hard night's work."

CHAPTER NINETEEN

Hickok hardly noticed the passage of time. He walked along morosely, his shoulders slumped, thinking of Priscilla Wendling and Milly Odum. He reviewed the tragedy over and over, replaying the events in his mind's eye to see if there wasn't something he could have done to prevent their deaths. But no matter how he considered the episode, he preceived there was no way he could have saved either woman. Still, guilt gnawed at his soul.

The gunfighter marched westward along winding valleys, over hills and mountains, constantly prodded by his captors to move faster. Geronimo tramped behind him, while Eagle Feather came last.

The realization that his wife and sons had been killed shattered the Flathead. Eagle Feather walked in a state of perpetual shock, his head bowed, rarely blinking, oblivious to the curses and shoves of the Breed.

Fatigue began to take its toll on Hickok. His leg muscles were aching terribly by nightfall. He'd anticipated the creatures would stop for the night, but they kept going, their animalistic physiques endowed with exceptional stamina.

The full moon rose in the east, casting its pale radiance over the land.

The cool night breeze revitalized the gunman. He breathed deeply and roused himself from his morbid introspection, shutting his mind to the memory of Priscilla and Milly being consumed by the vile mutations. He stared at the line of Bear People in front of him, then glanced back at the ten creatures bringing up the rear section. The sight of their brutish forms sparked a rare emotion.

Hatred.

Unadulterated, unmitigated hatred.

Ordinarily Hickok regarded enemies dispassionately. Fighting foes came with the job, and he seldom indulged in the luxury of exercising his personal feelings toward them. If Russians were the threat, he eliminated them coolly and efficiently, without becoming personally involved. Scavengers, drug lords, gangsters, androids, they were all the same to him. Line them up and he'd shoot them down. The number of adversaries didn't matter. Their lives were forfeit once they endangered the Family and the Home. And he'd killed countless enemies in the line of duty without feeling any animosity towards them whatsoever.

But not this time.

This was different.

Resentment dominated his being. He gazed at a trio of creatures who were bearing the bodies of the three dead mutations, and a tingle of pleasure ran down his spine at the thought of slaying every last one. If ever there had been opponents who truly deserved to die, the Breed definitely qualified.

Which brought him to the big question.

How to do it?

Hopelessly outnumbered and unarmed, Hickok knew he didn't stand a prayer unless he could get his hands on some guns. He guessed that his Colts had been left back on the hill where the fight took place, and he hoped Blade or Achilles had found the Pythons.

If they were still alive.

Blade's absence worried him. By all rights, knowing his giant friend as well as he did, Blade should have overtaken the Breed column already. Warriors were a loyal lot. They never deserted a fellow Warrior in a time of crisis.

Never.

Ever.

If Blade hadn't been killed, Hickok reflected, then the head Warrior would leave no stone unturned in his search for his friends. Granted, the Breed were trekking westward at a rapid rate, but Blade was no slouch in the speed department either, and the big guy could hike rings around most folks.

So where the blazes was he?

Hickok thought of Achilles, imagining how the greenhorn would react when he heard about Priscilla. Years ago, before Hickok had married Sherry, he had been in love with a woman named Joan, an excellent Warrior in her own right, and he recalled vividly the sorrow that had overwhelmed him when she was killed by the vicious Trolls in Fox, Minnesota. Achilles would probably feel the same way about the Mormon woman, and Hickok felt sorry for him.

He grinned.

Imagine that!

Feeling sorry for that pompous cow chip!

"What can you possibly find amusing at a time like this?"

The gruff question caused Hickok to look up in surprise.

Longat stood a few yards away. He fell in beside the gunman, studying Hickok's features. "I asked you a question."

"Get stuffed."

"Childish hostility is uncalled for."

"You're right," Hickok stated. "You deserve better than hostile words. You deserve to have your brains blown out."

The bear-man sighed. "Humans are so predictable. I foolishly believed we might have an intelligent discussion, but I should have known better."

"What do you want to palaver about?"

"Pala-what?"

"Why do you want to shoot the breeze with me?" Hickok

asked suspiciously.

"There are a few questions I need to ask."

"I figured as much."

"You did?"

"Yep. I was expectin' you to torture the information out of us."

Longat smiled. "How perceptive. Such treatment can still be arranged should you fail to cooperate."

"Fire up the brandin' irons."

"I don't understand."

The gunfighter smirked. "Get stuffed."

"You refuse to tell me what I want to know?"

"Bingo. You must have all the smarts in your family. You sure don't have the looks."

The mutation glowered for a moment, then unexpectedly chuckled. "Very well. We'll play this by your infantile rules. Since you won't meet me halfway, I'll call a halt and have the two Indians tied down and chopped into bits and pieces."

Hickok glanced down at the tomahawk in the creature's hairy right hand, thinking of the grisly death of Milly Odum. "You would too."

"Damn straight," Longat said. "As we have conclusively demonstrated, we of the Breed don't possess the inconsistent emotional weaknesses so prevalent in you humans."

"Yeah. I noticed. You're all rotten to the core."

"Be nice. What you refer to as rottenness is merely evidence of our superior will to survive. You regard us as callous brutes, when in reality we are simply treating you as you treat the lower animals. We categorically recognize human inferiority and relate to your kind accordingly."

"One of these days a human will cram those words right down your throat."

"Who? You?" Longat responded, and laughed. "You're totally in our power. Your life is in our hands." He paused. "And if you're thinking that your giant friend and the one in the red cloak will save you, think agin. They've been taken care of."

Hickok's pulse quickened. "They have?"

"Yes. I arranged a special reception for your friends in that rocky pass we went through last night. They're undoubtedly dead by now."

"Has your reception committe returned yet?"

"Not yet. Why?"

The gunfighter smiled. "Don't count your chickens until they're hatched, turkey."

Longat's eyes narrowed. "You have a lot of confidence in those two, I take it."

"In the big guy I do. He'll make mincemeat out of your precious Breed."

"The giant is formidable," Longat conceded. "He's already killed two of my people."

"I didn't blow away those three?" Hickok asked in surprise.

"You flatter yourself. No, you were responsible for slaying just one, which in itself is a remarkable feat. Our superior bodies can withstand more punishment than your frail human physiques."

"Are you sure you're not related to Achilles?"

"Who?"

"This guy I know. You and he have a lot in common. You're both so high on yourselves that your tootsies never touch the ground."

"I have nothing in common with a lowly human."

"Don't bet on it, buck-o."

The mutation gazed at the row of figures moving through the night. "By all rights I should have eliminated every one of you last night. We lost three good fighters and had four others injured. One of them is quite serious."

"Poor baby," Hickok said.

"Mock us while you can."

"I will."

Longat looked at the Warrior. "I intended to have the Flathead consumed next, but I might change my mind and take you."

"Don't do me any favors."

"Enough idle conversation. Where are you from, Hickok?

From other humans we've captured, I know about the general organization of the Federation. Your presence in this region indicates you hail from one of the factions, probably the Civilized Zone. Am I correct?''

The gunman didn't respond.

Longat hefted the tomahawk. ''Don't push me or the Indians will suffer.''

Hickok knew there was no other choice. He had to give in to the mutation's demands. But—and at the thought he almost snickered—there was no reason he had to tell the truth. ''Yeah. You're right. My pards and me are from the Civilized Zone.''

''Were you sent after us?''

''Yep.''

''I thought so,'' Longat declared with an air of conceit. ''Humans are blatantly transparent.''

''What else were you able to figure out?''

''I suspect that your friends and you are simply a scouting party sent ahead of the main force. I'd guess that a large contingent of troops is even now en route to Yellowstone. Am I right?''

''You're plumb amazing,'' Hickok admitted.

Longat smiled. ''Trying to thwart my heightened intellect is impossible. I deduced you were sent by the Civilized Zone after your little group disposed of those scavengers, and I realized a larger force would probably be arriving soon. That's one of the reasons I decided to return to our valley earlier than I'd originally planned. We're not ready to take on a Federation army yet. And when we do finally engage the Federation, I want it to be on our terms.''

''Where's this valley of yours?''

''Mars.''

''Geez. Don't you even know what planet you're on?''

''I admire a human who can retain his sense of humor when he's close to dying.''

Hickok idly gazed to the south, and in the distance he spied an immense body of water, its calm, mirrorlike surface reflecting the moonlight.

Longat looked in the same direction. "Yellowstone Lake."

"How do you know?"

"Because I consulted an old map of this territory before leaving our valley."

"You can read?"

"Keep it up."

"I do my best."

"What size is the force sent to find us?"

"Oh, a couple of regiments. About four thousand troops."

"That many?" Longat said. "What's the total size of the Federation Army?"

"Five hundred thousand soldiers."

"That's impossible!" Longat stated. "You're lying."

"I never fib to anyone, or anything, if it means my pards will buy the farm."

"But there can't be that many men in the entire Civilized Zone, let alone their Army. You'd have me believe millions of humans live in the Civilized Zone alone?"

"Afraid so."

"But the Flatheads we captured told us there are only ten thousand soldiers in the Civilized Zone Army."

"What do they know? The Flatheads are part of the Federation, but they're not experts on the Civilized Zone. How could they be? The ones you captured gave you their best guess, but I'm giving it to you straight. Why do you think I kept telling you the Federation will stomp your butts? Who cares if you double or triple your population? Even one hundred thousand of your kind won't be enough to lick the Federation," Hickok asserted, pleased at his performance, at the sincerity he managed to convey. Actually, he didn't have the slightest idea how big the Civilized Zone Army truly was, but he wanted to make the mutation sweat.

Longat pondered the information. "If the Federation is that powerful, I'll need to adjust my timetable accordingly. The Breed must become much stronger than I originally anticipated before launching our assault on the Federation."

"That'd be the smart move," Hickok agreed wholeheartedly.

"I need to verify your claim."

The gunfighter decided to change the subject. "My feet are killin' me. When are we going to stop for a break?"

"If we can maintain this pace, we'll halt tomorrow morning."

"I can hardly wait."

"Really? I wouldn't have expected you to be in such a hurry. Tomorrow morning we'll feast again. Perhaps I'll draw straws to determine if we should eat the Flathead or you."

Hickok made a show of scrutinizing the bear-man from head to toe. "If you ask me, you should give serious consideration to going on a diet."

CHAPTER TWENTY

"What is this place?" Achilles inquired.

"According to the map, this was once a tourist attraction known as Old Faithful," Blade replied.

"The geyser?"

"Yep."

They sat astride their horses on the cracked and pitted roadway that wound between several dilapidated wooden structures to their right and a flat expanse of barren earth on the left.

"Isn't this where Yeddt told us the Breed were heading?"

Blade nodded and turned his horse to the right, surveying the buildings for signs of habitation. From the condition of the partly collapsed roofs, the cracked walls, and the shattered windows, he surmised no one had occupied the facilities for decades. Dust covered everything. One of the buildings had once been a service station; the long-abandoned pumps were rusted out, their casings split. Another structure bore a barely legible sign on which the words FOOD and GIFTS could be distinguished.

"Do you think we beat them here?" Achilles asked.

"We should have. Even though we had to swing to the north to insure they wouldn't spot us, we pushed our animals hard enough to compensate for the added distance," Blade said. "All we can do now is take cover and hope they show up."

"I can't wait to see Priscilla again."

Blade rode around to the rear of the food and gift store and reined up. The asphalt parking lot behind the store was in slightly better shape than the road. Twenty yards from the rear door a crumbling, oxidized jeep rested on its hubs.

"I remember reading about Old Faithful during my schooling years," Achilles mentioned. "It's hard to believe millions of Americans traveled hundreds or thousands of miles to reach this very spot."

"What's so hard to understand?" Blade replied, dismounting. "Most Americans in the prewar era lived in towns or cities. They knew very little about nature and couldn't survive for two days in the wildneress on their own. There was no incentive for them to live off the land because all of their food was easily obtained in restaurants and markets. Their clothing could be bought at retail outlets. They had severed their ties to the ways of the natural world. Quite naturally, whenever they had the time, on vacations or whatever, they'd flock to the country to get a taste of the primal life." He scanned their surroundings. "They came here to escape the artificial world in which they lived."

Achilles slid to the asphalt. "I'm glad I didn't live back then."

Unslinging both the Commando and the Henry, Blade moved to the closed back door. He drew up his right leg, shifted, and delivered a side stomp kick to the peeling panel, fracturing the wood down the center. Half of the door fell inward. "Cover my back," he directed, and eased into the gloomy interior.

A narrow hallway, the floor caked with trash and dirt and the ceiling a haven for a variety of cobwebs, led past a closet, an office, and a storeroom to the front of the establishment. Debris littered the grimy tile underfoot. All of the shelves

were empty. The place had clearly been ransacked years and
years ago. Faded wrappers and rusty tin cans lined the aisles.
The big window facing the road and Old Faithful had been
broken into tiny shards.

Blade moved down an aisle to the front door, which hung
at a slant, attached to the frame by just its top hinge. He kept
clear of the doorway. Footprints in the dust would give them
away, and he wanted the Breed to draw well within the range
of his Commando. The closer, the better.

"Do you have a plan?" Achilles inquired.

"We'll hide out in here until they arrive, then play it by
ear. Our first priority is to rescue Hickok, Geronimo, and
the others. Once they're safe, we can concentrate on wiping
out the mutations."

"If the . . ." Achilles began, and abruptly stopped,
astounded by the sight across the road.

Attended by a muted crackling and a loud hissing, Old
Faithful erupted, sending a silvery spray of steaming water
high, high into the air. Attaining a height of 170 feet, the
water then fell back to the earth in a wide circular area around
the geyser, splattering silica in all directions.

"Wow!" Achilles said.

Blade watched the beautiful display in silence, thinking
of the irony involved. Once this geyser had drawn spectators
by the millions, and he remembered reading that scientists
and geologists had been concerned Old Faithful might stop
erupting, just like other famous geysers in Yellowstone.
Evidently, many geysers simply died out, lost their oomph,
after a while. But here was Old Faithful, continuing to
cascade water long after the millions of spectators had ceased
to exist.

The eruption lasted for several minutes. Then the hissing
abruptly ended and the last of the spray dropped to the soil.

"That was magnificent," Achilles commented. "Do you
think Yellowstone Park will ever be reopened?"

"Maybe one day the leaders of the Civilized Zone will
get around to it, after the scavengers and the mutants and
the raiders have all been exterminated."

Achilles sighed. "Then it will never reopen."

"Let's get comfortable," Blade suggested, and sank to his knees next to the bottom of the busted window, carefully avoiding the strewn glass.

"In case I should forget, I want to thank you again for the opportunity you've given me," Achilles remarked, unslinging the FNC and squatting alongside the giant.

"You can repay me by staying alive."

"I'll do my best. I want to live long enough to ask Priscilla to go back to the Home with us."

Blade glanced at the novice.

"I know I couldn't leave the Home, couldn't desert the Family. If she feels the same way about me that I do about her, then she might agree."

"It's worth a try," Blade acknowledged.

"Wouldn't it be funny? I mean, I came along to acquire combat experience, yet I may be going back with a treasure more valuable than any other. What's the thrill of combat compared to the genuine affection of a lovely woman?"

"Yep. You definitely should become a poet."

"I don't know the first thing about poetry, about putting words on paper."

"Plato once told me that poetry is the rhythm of the soul, not the rhyming of words."

Achilles chuckled. "I really must spend more time in Plato's company from now on."

They settled down to wait, placing the spare weapons on the tile near their legs. Thirty minutes passed. An hour. Ravens, jays, and an occasional hawk winged through the sky. Squirrels scampered in the trees and chipmunks frolicked among the boulders. Twice mule deer crossed their field of vision, and once four fat elk appeared in the forest on the opposite side of Old Faithful.

Blade savored the peace and quiet, knowing all too well what was coming. He double-checked the Commando, and wished he possessed ammo for the Henry and the Colts lying next to his right knee. His mind strayed, and he thought about his wife and son. Immersed in reflecting on the time he took

them on a vacation to a small lake north of the Home and
nearly got them all slain, he almost failed to register the
movement off to his left, to the east of the store. He casually
swung his head around and saw them.

The Breed.

The mutations were strung out in single file, advancing
down the center of the highway, hiking from the east toward
the geyser complex. One of them limped badly. Three others
were carrying the bodies of dead comrades.

Blade lowered his head below the sill and peeked over the
edge, counting the creatures. He stopped halfway through
his count when he spied Hickok, Geronimo, and Eagle
Feather marching along with their wrists bound. They
appeared to be extremely fatigued, and the Flathead's
expression was strangely dull, devoid of animation.

"Where's Priscilla?" Achilles inquired anxiously.

"I don't know," Blade whispered.

"Maybe she's at the rear of the column."

The rest of the Breed came into view, but the Mormon
woman wasn't with them.

"Dear Spirit!" Achilles breathed. "Where is she? What
could have happened to her?"

Blade's lips compressed as he studied the mutations. They
seemed to be tired too. Apparently the Breed had exerted
themselves to reach the site swiftly. They drew nearer until
they were directly in front of the store. He saw the creature
in the lead, the tallest mutation, halt, turn, and bark orders.
That must be Longat, he reasoned, and noticed that Longat
held Geronimo's tomahawk.

Many of the Breed sat down on the spot. Others stretched
or conversed. Hickok and Geronimo took a few steps to the
side, inadvertently moving closer to the store, and began
talking in hushed tones.

"Maybe Priscilla escaped," Achilles speculated. "Maybe
she's wandering around alone in the wilderness somewhere."

"Stop thinking about her."

"I can't."

"You have to concentrate on the task at hand," Blade

instructed him. "You can't afford to be distracted."

"I'll do my best."

Blade nodded and scrutinized the bear-men. His plan had worked to perfection. By discovering where the Breed were headed, he'd been able to get in front of the deviates. Now he could give them a taste of their own medicine. But how to do it without endangering Hickok and Geronimo? He needed a distraction. If the creatures could be diverted, it might be possible to get his fellow Warriors and the Flathead to safety. Exactly how to achieve the diversion puzzled him until he received an unexpected assist from Mother Nature.

Old Faithful erupted again.

Rumbling and hissing, the geyser spit its fountain of steaming water skyward.

The Breed predictably shifted to observe the spectacle. Every creature watched the rare display in fascination, some gesturing and chattering excitedly.

Blade rose higher, hoping Hickok and Geronimo would glance in his direction, but they both were glued to Old Faithful's performance, their backs to the store. The dummies. There would never be a better opportunity. "Stay put and cover me," he ordered, and darted out the front door.

Now if only none of the creatures turned around!

Blade raced toward his friends, constantly scanning the mutations, ready to fire if detected. He wanted to shout to get Hickok's and Geronimo's attention, but he'd also alert the Breed to his presence. Come on! he mentally shrieked. Look this way, you ding-a-lings!

Both the gunman and the Blackfoot continued to stare at the geyser.

Blade didn't know whether to grin or become furious. If he made it through this mess alive, he vowed to give the two of them a good swift kick in the seat of their pants for not maintaining an unflagging vigilance.

Then again, maybe he underestimated them.

Both Warrior's swiveled their heads, surveying the creatures, then each one took hold of Eagle Feather by an arm, pivoted, and took a stride in the direction of the store.

They simultaneously beheld the giant and both displayed fleeting amazement.

Blade halted ten yards from them, trained the Commando on the mutations, and motioned for them to hurry.

Beaming inanely, Hickok practically dragged the Flathead after him.

Geronimo kept pace, repeatedly glancing over his shoulder.

Old Faithful spewed more and more water into the air.

The Breed, still enthralled, watched.

Seven yards separated Blade from his friends. Five yards. He caressed the Commando's trigger, his whole body tense, certain the mutations would discover the strategem at any moment.

They did.

One of the Breed happened to idly look back at the buildings. Astonishment lined his bestial features for all of a second, until he opened his mouth and bellowed at the top of his lungs.

All of the mutations started to turn.

Blade dashed forward, letting his friends go past him. "Get inside!" he directed.

"About time you showed up, slowpoke," Hickok muttered, running toward the store where Achilles stood framed in the window.

There was no time for Blade to reply. He clasped the Commando firmly and cut loose, sweeping the barrel from right to left, mowing the Breed down, knowing from experience how difficult they were to kill and going for the head, seeing over a dozen craniums burst as heavy slugs tore through their heads from front to rear.

Voicing a commingled roar of rage and implacable animosity, the Breed charged the giant.

Blade deliberately held his ground. Hickok and Geronimo would need precious time so they could be cut free by Achilles, then grab their guns and reload if necessary, time he intended to supply. He poured a withering fire into the mutations, raking them with a hail of lead, keeping his finger depressed, pouring out every shot in his 90-round magazine, firing and firing until the machine gun went empty.

Fifteen of the creatures were prone on the asphalt or trying to rise, even though riddled with bullets. The rest surged in a frenzied wave at the Warrior.

Blade went to grab a fresh magazine, but he realized he'd never be able to insert it and draw back the cocking handle before the mutations reached him. And retreating to the store was out of the question. They'd catch him before he covered five yards. Stuck in the open, with nowhere to take cover, he did the only thing he could; he dropped the Commando, drew his Bowies, and attacked the Breed.

A few of the creatures stopped, taken aback by the sight of the lone giant rushing toward them. Their companions never slowed.

A smile on his lips, Blade met them in a savage clash, whipping the Bowies in a glittering onslaught, slashing and hacking and stabbing in a wild abandon, his body always in motion, always slicing and cutting, spinning and whirling, because he knew if he slowed for an instant they would seize him and overpower him with their greater numbers. Nails dug into his arms, shoulders, and thighs, and he ignored the pain and the stinging sensations, focusing exclusively on slaying the creatures, his arms whirlwinds of razor-edged death, severing hands and tearing open throats and rending faces in a mad melee of elemental ferocity.

Mutations fell right and left, their bloody forms dotting the tarmacadam.

Suddenly the Breed parted, and Blade found himself face to face with their leader, Longat. The creature snarled and swung the tomahawk, and Blade parried the blow with his right Bowie. Again Longat swung, his powerful sinews driving the tomahawk in a blow that would have smashed through the defenses of any ordinary man. But Blade's own bulging muscles were equal to the occasion, and he deflected the tomahawk. Again he warded off a swipe meant to cleave his skull, then again and again.

The mutations saw their chance. With the giant occupied,

they sought to encircle him and pounce on him from behind. One of them, skirting to the right, coiled his legs and was about to spring when a shot rang out. He collapsed in his tracks. The other creatures rotated in the direction of the rotort.

Hickok, Geronimo, and Achilles sprinted from the store, bearing to the left, intending to lure the mass of tightly packed bear-men away from Blade, leery of firing for fear of hitting the head Warrior. They succeeded beyond their highest expectations.

Every member of the Breed except for Longat ran toward the trio, growling and screeching, venting their wrath, eager to tear the humans limb from limb.

Hickok smiled as he saw the creatures moving away from Blade. The Breed had enjoyed the advantage the last time he'd fought them. They'd jumped him in the dark, using the cloak of night to their advantage. But this time the situation was different. This time they were fighting in broad daylight. This time he could see his targets clearly. He pressed the Henry to his right shoulder and levered off every round, aiming at their heads, felling a foe with every shot. The instant the Henry was empty, he let the rifle fall and resorted to his Colts, his hands a blur as he gripped the pearl handles and cleared leather. He heard Geronimo and Achilles firing, and then he opened up with the Pythons, every shot dead center.

Nearby, Achilles fought in a blind rage, the two words Geronimo had told him in the store resounding over and over in his mind. She's dead! She's dead! She's dead! And these sons of bitches had killed her. He expended every round in the Bullpup, let go, and pulled the Taurus and the Amazon. A creature loomed in front of him and he shot it between the eyes, then spun to blast another mutation. Coldly, methodically, he shot one after another, slashing at those who tried to rake him with their nails, holding his own, dominated by his fury, killing, killing, killing.

Only Geronimo had a breathing space. Fewer of the Breed came after him, and those who did he downed with the FNC.

Lacking firearms, the creatures were unable to close effectively, and Geronimo regarded their deaths as a virtual slaughter. He glimpsed Blade and Longat locked in combat, and he wished he was the one fighting the leader. He wanted to repay the deviate for taking his tomahawk. A bear-man sprang at him from the right, and he pivoted, the FNC bucking, stitching a pattern of crimson holes across the mutation's forehead. He turned and saw Blade slip on a puddle of blood.

Longat leaped forward, the tomahawk upraised, his lips curled back to expose his pointed teeth, his eyes gleaming points of ferocity.

Down on his right knee, Blade swept both knives upward to block the tomahawk. He could hear shooting, and he wanted to dispose of Longat quickly and aid his friend. To do so would require an unorthodox tactic, a move Longat wouldn't be expecting. As his shoulders absorbed the impact from the tomahawk, in a flash he perceived a means of gaining the upper hand.

Longat started to lift the tomahawk again.

Now! Blade reversed the grip on the Bowies, angled the bloody blades downward, and lunged, spearing a knife into each of Longat's feet, sinking both to the hilt.

The leader of the Breed stiffened and uttered a gurgling scream, then recovered and tried to swing the tomahawk, his movements awkward because his feet were pinned to the asphalt.

Blade was relentless. He straightened, his hands bunched into a single fist, and pounded the bear-man on the tip of the jaw, rocking Longat's head backward and crunching the creature's teeth together. Remorselessly, Blade struck with his fists in a flurry of battering punches, hitting Longat on the face, dazing the mutation. He thought of all the innocent lives the Breed had taken, all the people the mutations had eaten, and his visage acquired a stony cast. His huge fists rained on Longat. Rained and rained and rained.

Longat's nose was crushed, his lips battered to a pulp, and his cheeks split. He feebly attempted to employ the tomahawk, but a sledgehammer blow to his right eyebrow caused his arms to go limp and his body to sway.

Gritting his teeth, Blade tightened his right hand into a rock-hard fist. He slowly drew his arm back as far as he would go, then paused. "This is for the human race," he said, and swung with all of his might.

The force of the impact lifted Longat from his feet, actually tore the Bowies out of the ground and sent the bear-man sailing for over six feet to crash onto the tarmacadam, a crumpled wreck.

Blade abruptly became aware the firing had ceased and turned.

Eight yards away were Hickok, Geronimo, and Achilles. All three were staring at him somberly. Each one was spattered with crimson. Nineteen bearish corpses lay about them.

"Nice job," Geronimo said, stepping toward the fallen leader. "I just hope you didn't damage my tomahawk."

"Excuse me for living," Blade retorted, scanning the battlefield. "Why don't you mop up and make sure they're all dead."

"Let me," Achilles volunteered, hurring forward, his features grim. "I owe them," he added bitterly.

"Priscilla?"

Achilles frowned and shook his head.

"I'm sorry," Blade said, and looked at the normally loquacious gunfighter. "What's the matter? Nothing to say?"

Hickok twirled the Colts into their holsters, grinned, and nodded at Longat. "I love it when you get ticked off."

EPILOGUE

Blade found him standing on a small hill in the southeast corner of the Home. "So here you are. I've been looking all over for you."

Achilles turned slowly, his red cloak billowing in the stiff westernly wind, his countenance downcast. "Oh?"

"I thought you'd like to hear the good news. The Elders have formally accepted you as a Warrior."

"That's nice."

Blade studied the other man for a moment. "Don't jump for joy or anything."

"Sorry," Achilles said, and gazed off into the distance. "I keep thinking about her. The more I do, the more I realize how little I knew about her." He paused. "And yet, I cared for her so much."

"I know," Blade responded softly.

"Have you had any word about Eagle Feather?"

"Star says he's recovering slowly but surely. He suffered a tremendous loss, and he'll never be the same man he was before his loved ones were killed. But he's picking up the pieces."

"That's good," Achilles commented, and took a deep breath. "I appreciate all the effort you went to on my behalf. The Elders must have given you a hard time."

"Not at all, once Hickok and Geronimo reported on your performance during the mission."

"They did that for me?"

"Yep. They gave a glowing report. Your competence was never in question."

Achilles glanced at the giant. "Just my attitude."

"They know you've changed considerably since we got back a week ago. Everyone has noticed."

"So I'm not the pain in the ass I once was."

"You're just not as high on yourself."

The new Warrior pursed his lips and stared at the moat 40 yards away. "So which Triad will I be in? Are you going to shuffle the Warriors around?"

"No," Blade answeredc. "You'll be in Zulu Triad with Samson and Sherry. Samson is the head of your Triad and he'll be responsible for most of your training. He's one of the best. You'll be in good hands."

"I know his reputation."

Blade smiled. "And as if that's not enough, Hickok has graciously offered to teach you the fast draw."

"He what?"

"Apparently he saw you draw the Taurus during the battle with the Breed, and he described your draw as downright pitiful," Blade mentioned. "So he's taking it on himself to teach you how to pull a gun, as he put it, a mite faster than the speed of petrified molasses."

"Was I that bad?" Achilles asked in disbelief.

"No, but you know Hickok."

Achilles grinned. "Yeah. I'm beginning to think I do."

"You can take the rest of the day off and report to Samson first thing in the morning," Blade directed.

"Will do."

"If you think you need more time to yourself, just let me know."

"I'd only spend it moping," Achilles said. "At least I can keep busy with my new duties."

"I'll tell Samson to be expecting you at his cabin at daybreak," Blade said, and started to leave.

"Blade?"

The giant stopped. "Yeah?"

"Have you ever lost a woman you cared for deeply?"

"No, thank the Spirit. And I pray it doesn't happen. If I ever lose Jenny, I don't know what I'll do."

"I can imagine. I hope you never do."

"Thanks," Blade replied. "Did you know that Hickok lost a woman very dear to him about six years ago?"

"No, I didn't."

"Her name was Joan and she served as a Warrior."

"Was she killed in the line of duty?"

"Yep."

"How did Hickok take it?"

"As I recall, he cried his brains out, then crawled inside a shell for about a month. When he finally rejoined the human race, he was a much harder man than before," Blade related. "His marriage to Sherry was the best thing that ever happened to him. He's mellowed out since."

"Hickok cried? I thought he always has his emotions under control."

"Some grief is too deep for words and impossible to control."

"That reminds me," Achilles stated. "I'm coming with you."

"Oh?"

"Yeah. I want to look up Plato. Maybe some of his wisdom will rub off on me."

"The best teacher of wisdom is experience."

"There you go again. You sound like a blasted philosopher."

"And you're sounding like Hickok."

"I am?" Achilles replied, and his forehead creased. "Is that an insult or a compliment?"

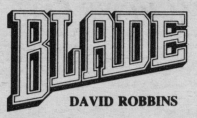